BALLOCK'S GUN WAS PRESSED TO THE BOY'S HEAD . . .

"I'll kill him!" Ballock shouted. "You come any closer and I'll kill him!"

The boy struggled like a rabbit caught in a trap but he was helpless in Ballock's grasp.

"Let him go!" Shiloh bellowed. "He's no part of this!"

But the rancher wasn't about to let his shield go. Instead, he dragged the boy forward, taking aim at Shiloh . . .

He could hear the boy screaming in fright, but he could also hear Ballock's hyena laughter, and that was most galling of all. Shiloh felt the sting of a bullet enter the flesh of his right buttock. He slapped his hand back, and when he brought it up before his eyes it was smeared with blood . . .

This book also contains a preview of Giles Tippette's exciting new western novel, *Sixkiller*.

Books in the SHILOH series by Dalton Walker

SHILOH
SHILOH 2: DESERT HELL
SHILOH 3: BLOOD RIVAL
SHILOH 4: THE HUNTED
SHILOH 5: HELL TOWN
SHILOH 6: SIDEWINDER
SHILOH 7: VENGEANCE TRAIL

SHILOH 8: BLOOD BOUNTY
(Coming in July)

SHILOH

VENGEANCE TRAIL

DALTON WALKER

DIAMOND BOOKS, NEW YORK

VENGEANCE TRAIL

A Diamond Book / published by arrangement with the author

PRINTING HISTORY
Diamond edition / April 1992

All rights reserved.
Copyright © 1992 by Charter Communications, Inc.
Material excerpted from *Sixkiller* by Giles Tippette
copyright © 1992 by Giles Tippette.
This book may not be reproduced in whole or in part,
by mimeograph or any other means, without permission.
For information address: The Berkley Publishing Group,
200 Madison Avenue, New York, New York 10016.

ISBN: 1-55773-690-1

Diamond Books are published by The Berkley Publishing Group,
200 Madison Avenue, New York, New York 10016.
The name "DIAMOND" and its logo are trademarks
belonging to Charter Communications, Inc.

PRINTED IN THE UNITED STATES OF AMERICA

10 9 8 7 6 5 4 3 2 1

1

SHILOH JERKED HIS battered Stetson down tight and used his spurs to fork his exhausted sorrel gelding into the teeth of the Nevada snowstorm. Ice crusted on his unshaven face and mane of scraggly blond hair. Somewhere hereabouts was the ranching and mining settlement called Chili Gulch, but damned if he could find it in this spring blizzard. Shiloh peered into the wall of flying snow and cussed. It wasn't supposed to do this in March and he was freezing right down to the marrow of his bones.

His situation, he knew, was quite desperate. The wind was howling and the temperature was at best zero, maybe even a lot colder when you factored in the killing wind. Shiloh gave himself another hour, maybe two, to find shelter. After that, it was simply a matter of whether he or his horse froze first. Something must have caught the attention of his horse because the animal's ears, which had been laid back, now flicked forward and the gelding altered its direction. Shiloh let the horse have its head, because *he* sure as hell hadn't a clue as to the best direction to travel.

The horse quickened its pace and Shiloh took heart until the animal stopped dead in its tracks.

"Well?"

Shiloh squinted into the driving snow, and when he could see nothing he spurred the horse a little ahead, and that's when he was almost knocked out of the saddle by the overhanging roof of a barn.

Shiloh dismounted and felt as if he were standing on columns of ice instead of his legs. He had no sensation in his feet and he hoped to hell they weren't frostbitten. Stumping forward, he found a handle to a door and pulled, but it was frozen shut. He grabbed the door with both hands and tore it open. Warm air, pungent with hay and horseshit, filled his nostrils, and he was practically run down by the gelding as it plunged headlong into the barn.

"Easy, damn you!" Shiloh snarled, pulling the door shut, then fumbling around in his Union army coat until he found some matches. He wasted two before he got a spluttering light going and held it aloft to see three other horses staring at him, steam pouring from their nostrils as they munched on hay.

Shiloh turned full circle, holding the match up high. The barn was about twenty feet square, and although it felt warm the temperature was still freezing because he could see ice coating the inside walls.

His sorrel, a big, ugly, half-starved beast with one white eye, charged the other horses with bared teeth and drove them away from the manger. The animal began to eat ravenously, half strangling because of the Spanish spade bit in its mouth. A palomino wheeled and kicked at the sorrel and Shiloh heard the hard pop of hoof striking flesh. The sorrel squealed and spun, big yellow teeth sinking into the palomino's shoulder, tearing flesh and opening up a deep wound. The palomino knocked another horse over trying to escape.

Shiloh watched with only mild interest. Horses, like dogs, humans or chickens, always had to establish a pecking order. In less than a minute this pecking order had been established, with his sorrel already the dominant animal.

Shiloh's match burned out and he lit another. This time he searched for a candle or lantern, but finding none he gathered a bit of old dried hay, twisted it into a torch and lit it. The hay burned fast and bright. Shiloh hurried over to the manger and tore off a board, then broke it over his knee and used it for kindling. Before the hay torch seared his hand he had started himself a campfire. It was going to get damned smoky in the barn, but he'd live with that.

Shiloh had a good-sized piece of gamy beef that was now frozen, and he used his bowie knife to scorch it over the fire. Before the ice crystals were melted inside the meat he wolfed it down, then reached into his saddlebags for a bottle of cheap whiskey. Between the fire, burned meat and bad liquor, Shiloh began to feel half alive again. When the smoke became so thick he started to wheeze, Shiloh opened the door of the barn. The howling wind quickly drove the smoke out through the cracks in the barn walls. Shiloh stood in the doorway and wondered if he should try and find a house or if he should just wait out the storm in the company of these horses.

Problem was, he had no idea of the direction to take to find a house. And a man on foot, lost in a hard blizzard like this, would be a goner in less than thirty miles. Shiloh slammed the barn door. To hell with it, he thought. He would try to get some sleep. Maybe when he woke up the storm would be over, or at least eased up enough to show the direction he ought to be headed.

Sleep came easy to Shiloh. It always did. The hard part was the recurring dreams he suffered, and they usually came when he was totally exhausted. As always, he would see himself as a young, thin and frightened Union soldier. The dreams were peopled with gory, ghastly faces, and the sky and the battleground were a crimson wash. Usually, the dreams had him standing among the dead and the dying, an empty rifle in his fists. Overhead, thunder would roll in chorus with cannon and then it would start to rain. A cold, chilling rain that washed the crimson from the land, leaving the dead as pale as snow, with black eyes that stared accusingly at Shiloh from the darkest recesses of hell. At that point, Shiloh would snap awake, drenched in a fearful sweat.

"Get up, damn you!" a voice cried, splitting the nightmare. "Get up or I'll blow your thievin' head off!"

Shiloh blinked and found himself gazing into the barrel of a gun. His eyes followed the barrel up an arm, then a body, to the face of a large, bearded man with deep-set, merciless eyes. Eyes that made Shiloh reach for his gun.

"I took it, you thievin' bastard."

"I haven't taken a damn thing from this place," Shiloh argued. "What's to take in a freezing old barn!"

"You let your horse eat our hay. Hay is damned expensive this time of year. You got ten dollars to pay for the hay your horse ate?"

"Ten dollars! Why, mister, ten dollars is worth more than he'd eat here in a month!"

The man cocked back the hammer of his six-gun. "You're a thief. I just gave you a chance to settle, but you're not willing to do what's right so I guess you'll have to pay."

Shiloh sat up with a shake of his head. This wasn't yet as bad as his recurring battlefield dreams, but it was quickly moving in that direction.

"Listen, mister," Shiloh tried to explain, "I got caught in the blizzard and my horse just brought me to this shelter and saved our lives. I been here no more than three, maybe four hours. As soon as the storm passes, I'll be moving on."

"Maybe you will," the man said, "and maybe you won't. That'll depend on how we decide to punish a thief."

"I told you I'm not a thief!" Shiloh said, growing angry.

In response, the man pistol-whipped him across the forehead. Shiloh felt blood cascade down his face and his vision turned scarlet. He cursed and then tried to lunge forward to grab his tormentor but he was pistol-whipped to his knees.

The man grabbed his hair and twisted it hard. "Get up, thief!"

Shiloh was hauled to his feet. He was too dazed to offer a fight, and the next thing he knew he was being propelled out the doorway.

The hard, freezing wind washed away the fog in his mind and cleared his senses. He was being shoved through the curtain of driving snow and then suddenly his head was banging against a door.

The door opened and Shiloh was thrown to the floor. He tried to stand, but the man with the gun buried a boot between his legs. Shiloh gagged and rolled over onto his side, knees drawn up to protect his manhood from further abuse.

"Look at the thief I found in our barn! Sonofabitch drove off our horses so that his own could fill its belly."

"That isn't true!" Shiloh argued, looking at the other two men and recognizing that they were all brothers. The trio were thick-chested, brutal-faced bastards. Shiloh knew enough about hard men to see that reason or mercy was not in their make-up.

"The hell it ain't! And Clete, that palomino of yours looks like it fell on a bear trap. Got a bad shoulder now. Probably never be sound again. His horse done took a hunk of meat out of the palomino, I tell you."

"Sonofabitch!" Clete cursed. "That was my favorite horse!"

"It was your *only* horse," the third man growled. "What's the stranger ridin'?"

"A big, ugly sorrel gelding. Ain't near as good as the palomino was before it was ruint."

"How much money you carryin', stranger?"

Shiloh swallowed the gorge rising in his throat and managed to say, "Less than ten dollars."

"Not enough. My palomino was worth thirty."

"He's worth no more than twenty!" Shiloh protested.

"I said thirty!"

The three brothers exchanged glances and Shiloh knew they were deciding to kill him. Right now, they were just toying with him like a cat would a helpless mouse. Shiloh figured if he was going to die, he'd go down fighting.

"What else did this thief have, Matt?"

"A pretty good set of matched Colts and a double-barreled shotgun."

"No rifle?"

"Nope. Just the scattergun. Looks to be in good condition, though."

"It is," Shiloh muttered. "The shotgun is worth more than that palomino. Those matched Colts are worth more than a hundred dollars."

"Looks like you lose out," Matt said, winking at Clete and the third brother, whose name Shiloh had not yet heard.

"What are you going to do to me?" Shiloh asked, coming to his feet.

"Well, sir," Matt said, grinning at his brothers, "if the weather was nice, we'd hang you for thievin', but since it ain't nice, I guess a bullet will have to do."

Shiloh's head was still spinning and he knew that he was a dead man if he tried to fight or escape before he cleared his senses. What he needed was a little time—and a diversion. Something, anything, to distract these three from their murderous purpose.

"Why don't you take the gold in my saddlebags?" he blurted.

"Gold?" Clete's eyes snapped to Matt. "Didn't you even check his saddlebags?"

"Well, no, but . . ."

Clete dismissed his brother and turned his full attention back to Shiloh. "Mister, how much gold you got in them bags? Could be we'll let you buy your life after all."

"I've nearly five hundred dollars' worth," Shiloh said. "I brought it over from the Comstock Lode. Took me a year to dig that much paydirt."

"You don't look like a miner to me," Clete said, turning to the youngest brother. "Jess, does he look like a miner or prospector to you?"

"No, sir," Jess said. "I don't know what he looks like except a thief."

Shiloh could see now that Clete was at the top of this pecking order. His brothers would follow his orders.

"Matt, go back out there and bring in them saddlebags."

"He's probably lyin' through his damned teeth," Matt said. "I already gone outside once. Damn near froze to death. If you want them saddlebags, send Jess."

Clete didn't like being talked back to but he said, "All right, Jess, go and get 'em. We'll wait."

Jess was the smallest and youngest of the three. And being the youngest, he was also the most careless. As he moved toward the door, Jess stepped between his brothers and Shiloh. It was the opportunity Shiloh needed. Cat-quick, he jumped forward to loop his arm around Jess's throat and then tear the six-gun from his holster.

"Drop those guns or he's a dead man!"

Matt and Clete didn't drop their guns but held them steady on Shiloh while Jess struggled helplessly. Shiloh choked him down harder and Jess began to gag and thrash.

"Your play!" Shiloh cried. "Drop the guns or I either break the kid's neck or I put a bullet in his head."

"Do that," Clete hissed, "and you're a dead man yourself."

Matt nodded. "If we drop our guns, then you got us all. No, sir! What we have here appears to be a Mexican stand-off, but we're holding more cards. Your play, mister."

Shiloh knew the two older brothers weren't bluffing. "I'm leaving," he said, wondering how he was going to hold Jess around the throat, keep his gun trained on Clete and Matt, and also open the door. "All I want is out of here. No cause for blood to be spilled."

Clete and Matt said nothing because they could see that Shiloh would find it impossible to open the door without taking the barrel of his gun off them. Shiloh's mind raced and he saw only one chance. He pulled and dragged Jess along the wall until his back was to the cabin's lone glass window. Then he slammed his elbow through the glass. Snow and wind blasted into the cabin, half blinding everyone with demented fury.

"Damn you!" Matt shouted, firing in anger and hitting his young brother in the shoulder.

Jess cried out and Shiloh fired at Matt, putting a bullet into his gut an instant before Shiloh dragged Jess backward through the shattered window. He and Jess struck the frozen ground, then Shiloh released the wounded man and ran in the direction he hoped was the barn. Behind him, he heard gunshots and curses.

Shiloh found the barn and opened the door. He stepped behind it and saw Clete appear as an apparition from the driven snow. They both fired at the same instant. Clete's bullet plowed into the door but Shiloh's bullet struck Clete in the neck. The man screamed and grabbed his throat, but nothing could have stopped the blood from spraying across the snowy ground as Clete staggered around and around, drowning to death on his feet.

Shiloh could have let the man bleed or choke to death on blood, but he was not a vindictive or cruel man, so he mercifully shot Clete through the heart before he slammed the barn door shut and collapsed to his knees. Shiloh was covered with his own blood from Matt's vicious pistol-whipping. He was also sick to his stomach from the kick he'd taken in his crotch. His only consolation was that Matt was gut-shot and dying slow in the freezing cabin.

As for young Jess, well, that one could either bleed to death or wander off into this damned Nevada blizzard and take his chances. Shiloh wasn't going to spend more than a few minutes in this barn to clear his head. After that, he was going back to the cabin and he'd damn sure clean house. Shiloh waited about ten minutes for his nausea to pass, then he yanked his scattergun out of his saddle boot and headed back to the cabin. When he entered, Jess was gone and Matt was still dying with a slug in his belly. Shiloh knelt beside the poor bastard that had kicked and pistol-whipped him so savagely. "How does it feel, big man?"

"Rot in hell!"

"Maybe I will someday, but not until you've burned there a good long while first."

Matt cursed and Shiloh turned his back on the man and examined the contents of the shack. He found a blanket, which he used to cover the broken window to keep out the snow and most of the wind. Shiloh lit a candle and found a bottle of whiskey. He smacked his lips and consumed the liquor in great gulps.

"Ahhhh!" he growled as the fire seared its way down his gullet to his gut. "Damn that does good on a miserable day like this!"

"Give me some!" Matt croaked, raising his hand.

Shiloh looked down at the dying man. "I don't believe I will."

"Damn you, it's mine!"

"*Was* yours," Shiloh said. "Remember? I'm a thief. And I just stole this bottle for myself. Sorry."

Matt cursed again and tried to rise, but the effort made him vomit and he choked himself to death.

Shiloh studied the room. It was a pig sty but he did see good saddles, rifles and outfits. Things that he would transport to Chili Gulch or some other town and sell. Yes, Shiloh thought, it had been a hard, violent day, but also a very profitable one, and that was about as much as any bounty hunter could ever expect.

2

THE STORM PASSED two days later, and when it broke the sun burned through the clouds and the snow glistened and melted. During his waiting time, Shiloh forayed out into the yard searching for a frozen mound that would signify the body of Jess. But he never found the expected frozen corpse, and whatever tracks Jess had made were scrubbed out by the wind.

"If he somehow made it to Chili Gulch," Shiloh said to himself, "that might cause me problems."

Restless and low on food, Shiloh saddled his own horse along with the other three. He tied them all together with a long lead line and left nothing of value in the cabin save the furniture, stove, and planks. Shiloh figured he could get maybe ten dollars for the injured palomino and fifteen or twenty for the other two horses. Add to that the value of the saddles, tack, weapons, bedrolls and other items he'd packed, canvased, and lashed down tight, and Shiloh knew he'd make himself several hundred dollars.

Of course, if there were questions of ownership, perhaps he'd do better to ride south toward the more distant

Tuscorora. But the thing of it was, Shiloh was a man of principle, and he shared no guilt in the deaths of Matt and Clete. They'd abused him and they'd have murdered him if he hadn't killed them first. As for young Jess, well, Shiloh was not a vengeful man. If he saw Jess on the trail, he would not try to kill him outright. He would give the young man the chance to walk away in peace and perhaps even grow old. Shiloh did not enjoy killing, it was all business. To his way of thinking, you killed for only two reasons—self-preservation and money.

It was still below freezing and the sun was having a tussle with the clouds when he rode out of the yard. Shiloh was pretty sure that Chili Gulch was due west and so he prodded the sorrel along and tried to ignore the pained grunts of the limping palomino as it dragged up the rear of their little caravan. That afternoon, the wind picked up sharply and Shiloh cussed under his breath because he could see that there was another damned storm brewing. But an hour later, he also saw Chili Gulch.

It was about as pathetic as most settlements in the west, with three or four saloons, two large hotels, a half dozen businesses and a collection of shacks mixed with one or two decent brick houses where the monied people of the town lived. At the east end of the town Shiloh saw a big livery with several large pole corrals filled with horses, oxen and mules. It was to be his first stop and Shiloh hoped the market was good for horses because he was near broke and in bad need of rest, food and ammunition. His sorrel was showing ribs and its shoes were as thin as paper. Shiloh knew that if he did not get it shod, the sorrel would throw a shoe and probably go lame.

He rode down from the sagebrush hills with a cold wind in his face. His nose and eyes ran and he felt hungry, tired and generally miserable. Chili Gulch, even as sorry-looking as it appeared, would offer a hot bath. Shiloh cheered his flagging spirits by promising himself a very hot bath, a bottle of good whiskey and a bad woman—in just that order.

When Shiloh reached the livery, he dismounted, tied the horses and peered into the dim recesses of the barn.

"Hello in there!" he called.

"Hello yourself!" a voice grumped from the shadows before stepping out into sunlight.

The man was old, small and lopsided. He walked with a bad limp and one shoulder slumped. He was silver-bearded and wore an old derby hat, red flannel shirt and suspenders made from a pair of rawhide reins. He wasn't barefooted, but his shoes were so worn through that he might just as well have been.

Shiloh said, "Is this your place?"

"Afraid so. What do you want?"

"I got three horses and saddles to trade or sell. You buying or do I ride on to the next town?"

"You can do whatever the hell you want," the man growled, spitting a stream of tobacco close enough to splash Shiloh's boots.

Shiloh took an immediate disliking to this man. Had he and the sorrel gelding not been so damned thin and worn down, Shiloh would have climbed back into the saddle and ridden on. But hunger and weariness made him a little more inclined to negotiate.

"You want to make an offer or not?" he asked, gesturing toward the animals. "I'm in the mood to sell if you're willing to make a reasonable offer."

The liveryman cackled. " 'Reasonable'? Now that word has caused more businessmen to go broke than any other, 'cept maybe the word *credit*. And I'll tell you somethin', stranger, I don't give credit and I don't make money bein' 'reasonable.' "

"The hell with you," Shiloh said, turning back toward his sorrel. "I don't aim to be giving these horses and good saddles away."

The liveryman cleared his throat. "Nobody said anything about gettin' anything for nothin'. On the other hand, that's what you paid for them three horses, ain' it?"

Shiloh tightened his cinch. "What do you mean?"

"I mean that it looks damn funny for a man to be leading around saddled horses loaded with bedrolls, canteens and rifles. Seems to me that you musta took 'em from three men."

Shiloh expelled a deep breath. "You got something to say, say it plain or shut up."

"What I'm sayin' is that I know the men that owned them horses. You either stole 'em, won 'em at cards or somehow killed those three brothers and took the horses for yourself."

"Take your pick," Shiloh said. "It don't matter to me what you think because the horses are mine."

"You got a bill of sale?"

"Nope."

"Then you're askin' to be invited to your own necktie party."

"Mister," Shiloh said, mounting his horse, "you talk way too damn much."

He started to rein off toward the center of town but the liveryman stepped into his path. "Hold up there, damn you! I never seen a man so impatient to get himself in trouble as you are. Don't you know that the three brothers who owned those horses ride for the Lazy B ranch?"

"I don't know anything about any Lazy B ranch," Shiloh said. "Those three horses aren't even wearing a brand."

"Maybe not, but they're known in these parts, as are the brothers who rode 'em. And if you want to parade them horses down the main street of Chili Gulch and have some of the other Lazy B riders see 'em and decide to lynch you from the nearest cottonwood tree, why you just go right on ahead. Ride off, mister. Get your neck stretched."

"Maybe I'll just find myself another town," Shiloh said.

"Maybe you won't reach it if the blizzard gets any worse or if word gets out about what you done."

"Is that a threat?" Shiloh asked quietly.

"It's a promise," the liveryman said, hitching up his suspenders. "You either sell the whole kit and kaboodle to me, or you are in more trouble than you can handle. Which is it going to be?"

Shiloh had a powerful urge to draw his gun and kill the old sonofabitch who was obviously blackmailing him. However, killing the man would no doubt bring folks running, and then he'd have to abandon the three horses and wind up with nothing but a posse on his heels. Given the shape he and his sorrel were in, Shiloh figured he'd have damn little chance of outrunning anything faster than a kid on foot.

"How much?"

"Fifty dollars for everything—weapons included."

"What! Why the guns and rifles alone are worth far more than that!"

"Not if word gets out where they came from." The liveryman stepped closer. "Look at it this way, friend. If you won everything fair and square, you can say no to me and sell your bounty elsewhere. But if you killed them three Lazy B riders, you can sell everything to me, pocket fifty dollars cash and ride out of Chili Gulch with better than a month's wages and no posse on your tail. Tuscorora is sixty miles south."

Shiloh looked outside at the approaching storm. "I'm played out," he said. "My horse won't make it another sixty miles without shoes and some rest and grain."

"Then take the fifty dollars."

Shiloh hated to be taken advantage of, but his back was to the wall because that shrewd old bastard had him pegged right.

"Fifty dollars and you board my sorrel as long as I feel like staying in Chili Gulch. And you feed him like he was a damned elephant."

The old man scratched his beard. "You'd be far better off tradin' the sorrel for one of my good horses and then ridin' out the minute the storm breaks."

"I've ridden about as far as I can go for now," Shiloh said. "And if that next storm I see on the horizon is going to be as nasty as she appears, then I'd get caught in another damn blizzard and they'd find your damned fifty dollars on my frozen corpse."

"All right," the man said. "Fifty dollars and board for the sorrel for one week. After that, it's a dollar a day for hay. Quarter extra if you want a boy to curry and grain the animal, which it sure as hell could stand."

"Let's see the color of your money, old-timer." Shiloh dismounted. He was really getting shafted on this deal. "I don't take any Mexican or Confederate money. I want greenbacks or gold."

"It'll be gold dust. But first, let's get these horses inside before someone sees 'em. That happens, our deal is off."

"How are you going to get rid of 'em if they're so damned dangerous?"

"I got friends who will take them out tonight after dark, saddles and all. They'll sell 'em up in Gold Creek."

"And you'll make a pile of money?"

The liveryman shrugged his narrow shoulders. "It'll help," he admitted, "but my friends don't work cheap, so I won't be livin' high and mighty."

"On fifty dollars," Shiloh grumped, "neither will I. Where's the best place to stay in this town?"

"There's two hotels, the Ambassador and the Bonanza. I was you, I'd stay at the Ambassador, and I'd do my drinkin' at the Idaho Saloon."

"Why?"

"All the Lazy B cowhands stay at the Bonanza, and the only saloon they don't drink and raise hell in is the Idaho."

"Something wrong with the place?"

"The Idaho has the worst whiskey in Chili Gulch, its owner is an ill-tempered sonofabitch and his prices are too damned high."

"Great," Shiloh growled. "Any other reasons I should drink there?"

"Nope."

After they got the horses inside and penned up in the shadowy stalls, the man handed Shiloh a poke of gold dust. "By the way," he said, "my name is Isaac, and remember we never did business except for me boardin' that poor sorrel gelding of yours."

"I understand." Shiloh turned to leave.

"You bury all three deep?" Isaac called.

"Nope."

"What the hell does that mean?"

"Means the ground is frozen, you old fool. Means I only killed two. The one named Jess got away but he's wounded. Might have frozen in the storm. Might have reached help. Doesn't much matter to me one way or the other."

Isaac began to cuss and raise hell but Shiloh didn't stop walking. He had fifty dollars' worth of gold dust and his horse was in good hands. If Jess was to be a problem, Shiloh would face that when it came and not a minute sooner. Until then, fifty dollars would go a long way in a sorry little town like Chili Gulch.

3

THE SNOW WAS starting to fly again when Shiloh entered the warm and spacious lobby of the Ambassador Hotel. There was a big potbellied stove that was so hot its metal was cherry pink. The stovepipe that lifted through the side of the back wall clanked and banged like the pots and pans in a drummer's traveling wagon. There were about ten chairs that ringed the stove, every one of them occupied by men smoking, talking and generally taking their ease.

Shiloh had not been really warm in a good long time. His hands were numb and his feet were blocks of ice. Wiping his running nose with the back of his sleeve, he went directly to the hotel desk and rang a bell. His appearance stopped conversation and everyone craned their necks to study him a moment before they resumed their conversations.

Shiloh rang the bell again, and when it brought no response he said angrily, "Anybody know if the damned desk clerk is asleep or drunk?"

A short, barrel-chested man rose from one of the chairs and with a look of extreme annoyance, marched stiffly across the lobby to take his place behind the registration desk. "I ain't either one," he snapped. "Rooms are ninety cents a night. If you want clean sheets and a wool blanket, that costs an extra ten cents. If you want a hot bath, that'll be another two bits. Soap is a nickel."

"Well for cripes sakes!" Shiloh complained. "Do you also charge extra for the towels?"

"Yep. Another nickel."

Shiloh yanked his poke of gold dust from his pocket. "I'll take the works for . . . oh, a week I guess."

"That'll be nine forty-five, you might as well round it off to ten dollars."

"The hell with that," Shiloh said, his voice flat and hard. "Weigh the dust and I'll be watching."

The hotel clerk didn't like Shiloh one bit. He might have even tried to cheat him, but there was a big sign behind the gold-dust scale guaranteeing it was accurate and that the current price of gold was twenty-five dollars an ounce. For his own part, Shiloh was not an especially generous man, and he detested the idea of being cheated by some surly desk clerk.

"Sign the book," the clerk ordered, reaching for a key. "You'll have room two-fourteen. Second door on your right."

"Is it warmed up?"

" 'Course not! Do you expect us to heat empty rooms in this freezing weather? But there's a little wood-burning stove in there and it'll heat up fast."

"Is there kindling wood up there?"

"Nope. Cost you another fifty cents."

Shiloh's hand streaked across the registration desk. He grabbed the clerk by the shirtfront and hauled him up on his toes. "Mister," he said, "either you keep me in wood or I'm going to burn your damned mattress and furniture! Now which is it!"

"All right! All right!" the man cried. "I'll send up free wood."

"Now! And a hot bath!"

"Sure. After all, you just paid for one every day."

"That's right," Shiloh said, releasing the man. "And have someone put my gear in the room too."

He turned his back on the clerk and strode over to the clerk's empty chair near the potbellied stove. Shiloh flopped down in the chair and kicked his feet out so they were right next to the metal. Almost immediately they began to steam and stink.

"Jaysus!" one of the men complained. "Mister, either the soles of your feet are crusted with cow shit, or else you got the dirtiest feet this side of St. Louis!"

Shiloh twisted his chair to regard the man. "I'm ice cold and hungry. I need whiskey and a woman and a hot bath. I'm mean and out of patience. Unless you want me to shove your head into that stove, you better keep your mouth shut. Understand?"

Shiloh was not a huge man. Not much taller or heavier than average, but with his scarred and bloodied face revealing a pair of hard, uncompromising gray eyes, he looked wild and dangerous. The man who had spoken swallowed nervously and tried to smile.

"Didn't mean nothing by what I said, stranger."

"Of course you did! My feet *do* stink, but so do yours and every other man's in this lobby."

The man nodded vigorously. He got up and hurried toward the stairs, shot Shiloh a look of hatred, then rushed upstairs.

"Dumb sonofabitch," Shiloh muttered, pulling his Stetson low on his eyes and reveling in the heat that was just starting to move from his feet up through his entire body. "Damn, it feels good to thaw!"

No one dared to comment. They just stared at Shiloh and after a little while, one by one, they got up and left the lobby until Shiloh was alone. He chuckled, knowing he was the cause of their leaving. That was just fine. Shiloh was a man who preferred his own company anyway.

After his feet really began to smoke, Shiloh stood up and walked outside. The cold didn't seem so bad now that he had thawed out a little, but the next blizzard was almost upon them and the snow was flying again. Shiloh turned and headed down the icy boardwalk toward the Idaho Saloon.

There were just three patrons and an immense bartender, who stood at least six inches taller than Shiloh. He was bald, and an unlit cigar protruded from the corner of his mouth. He might have been forty, but Shiloh judged him a few years older.

"Whiskey," Shiloh said, edging up to the bar.

"Whiskey it is," the man rumbled, setting a dirty glass on the bartop and spilling it full of cloudy liquor.

"To your health," Shiloh said, raising the glass and gulping the whiskey down. The liquor was horrible. It was worse than drinking pure kerosene, and it seared Shiloh's poor throat all the way to his belly, where it bubbled like witches' brew and made him gag.

"Wow!" Shiloh wheezed. "Where did you get that particular brand of tarantula juice!"

"I brew it myself," the bartender growled menacingly. "What's the matter? Don't you like it?"

"Sure!"

"Then you'll have another?"

Shiloh managed to nod his head. The second drink went down a little easier. Perhaps the first drink had numbed his gullet and his gut so that it didn't burn so bad.

The bartender was pleased. "You're a pretty good man to drink that stuff straight."

"I am?"

"Sure! Just me and a few others can drink it straight without some water."

"How about that!" Shiloh choked with tears filling his eyes.

"This one is on the Idaho," the giant said, pouring Shiloh a third glass and himself one as well. "To health and wealth."

The giant raised his glass and Shiloh reckoned he had better do the same. They drank and Shiloh knew that he'd had enough.

"Got a bath waiting for me at the Ambassador," he managed to say.

"Need a woman to go with it?"

"Wouldn't mind."

"Good. You pay me two dollars and I'll see she scrubs your back and whatever else you want scrubbed."

Shiloh did not want to insult or anger the giant so he paid.

"You come back now!" the bartender called as Shiloh swayed outside, feeling as if a gong was ringing inside his head.

Shiloh waved, and when he got outside he grabbed a porch post, leaned out in the street and vomited the whiskey, sure that it was poison and that he'd go blind or crazy if he didn't rid his belly of the vile stuff.

"Lazy B riders or not," he muttered as he staggered back to the Ambassador Hotel, "that's the last time I'm drinking his whiskey."

Shiloh had a good afternoon. The girl was warm and willing and the bath was hot. After she left, he shaved and found a clean shirt, then went downstairs and inquired about places where a man could find a steak dinner. There were only two choices but they were both decent.

That evening the wind began to howl in earnest, and nothing in its right mind moved outside as the Nevada blizzard struck Chili Gulch hard enough to shake the walls and rattle the windows. Out in the hills tents blew away, leaving prospectors to either freeze or fight their way into town and huddle by the fire.

The storm lasted three days and nights, and when it blew off it left Chili Gulch buried under a blanket of snow almost four feet deep. There was no way out and no way in, but as long as the whiskey, firewood and food held out, no one seemed to give a damn. Shiloh did not make friends around the potbellied stove, despite the many hours he spent warming himself. The other hotel boarders seemed to understand that he was not a man who cared much about cattle, mining, or commerce. He would expound on guns, horses and outlaws.

"I wear two guns and prefer a cross draw because that's how I learned how to shoot," he explained one evening to the group around the stove. "And there are times when one Colt and six bullets just isn't enough to get the job done."

"Mister," a short balding man named Thatcher, who was the local gunsmith, said, "I never seen the time when one gun, properly handled, couldn't eliminate every kind of grief that a man will run across on the western frontier."

"Well," Shiloh said, "you're entitled to your opinion. I hear that you're a very good gunsmith, so I respect your thoughts, but you're not in my line of business, and when it comes to trouble you don't know diddly-squat."

The gunsmith blinked and his face flushed with anger. "Maybe I don't know about shooting other men and maybe you're sayin' you do."

"That's exactly what I'm saying," Shiloh told them all. "I'm a bounty hunter and I don't make excuses. I hunt outlaws for money. Somebody has to do it because out here the law is stretched way too thin."

"Blood money! That's what you are takin' when you kill a man for the bounty on his head," Thatcher railed.

"It can be blood money," Shiloh admitted, refusing to get riled by the gunsmith's holier-than-thou attitude. "But on the other hand, it should be understood that I always give those I hunt a chance to surrender peaceably. If they do, I treat 'em fair until they're in the hands of the law."

"But if they don't, you gun them down."

"That's right," Shiloh said, his voice hardening with impatience. "And you need to understand, sir, that by gunning them down, I'm probably saving their next victim's life."

Thatcher wasn't a bit impressed by Shiloh's logic. "You don't know that for sure!"

"No," Shiloh admitted, "I do not. However, I think most everyone here would agree that the kind of men that have bounties on their heads aren't the kind to suddenly get religion and become model citizens."

Shiloh's comment caused several of the boarders to chuckle, and even the gunsmith had to nod his head in reluctant acceptance. "I still say," he argued, "that a man who would kill other men for money is going to be judged hard by the Lord on his day of reckoning."

"The Lord?" Shiloh asked innocently. "Why, I'd be willing to bet that everyone in this room will serve some hard time in hell. Not a single one of you is a candidate for sainthood."

"But we never killed for money!"

"No," Shiloh admitted, "but then some of us have quicker hands and stronger stomachs than others. And if I save the life of a man or woman who would have died by the hand of an outlaw, then it seems to me that it all balances out. I take a life—in return I save a life."

Many of them nodded their heads in agreement because Shiloh's reasoning made good, hard sense when you looked at it in that particular way. The gunsmith, however, was not convinced. " 'Thou shalt not kill!' It's one of the Bible's holiest commandments."

" 'An eye for an eye and a tooth for a tooth,' " Shiloh countered. "And 'judge not lest ye be judged.' "

The gunsmith shook his head, climbed out of his chair and left in a huff.

Shiloh frowned. He reached into his pocket and found the makings for a cigarette, which he rolled. Licking the paper, he said to no one in particular, "Sitting around here with you boys is about to bore the ass off me. Where can a man find an honest poker game in this one-horse town?"

"Delta Saloon always has a couple of games."

"And how is their whiskey?"

"Compared to what?"

"That poison that the Idaho sells."

"The whiskey at the Delta isn't made in the back room. It comes all the way from Tuscorora and it's pretty damn good. As for the rest of it, be warned there's a hard crowd at the Delta."

"A hard crowd?" Shiloh said. "That doesn't worry me much."

"Didn't expect it would," the man said, "but a fella is as likely as not to get cheated or his butt whipped by the Lazy B cowboys that hang out in the Delta."

"It's a free country," Shiloh opined. "A man ought to be able to play poker or have a decent glass of whiskey wherever he wants."

As Shiloh headed for the Delta, it occurred to him that he was being pigheaded. If he had any sense, he'd avoid the Delta and the Lazy B cowboys, but taking the easy way out just was not his natural style. When he stepped into the Delta, a thin, unsmiling brunette was playing a piano and trying to sing, but she was no better than a catamount howling at the moon and everyone was ignoring her.

Shiloh bellied up to the bar and ordered a whiskey.

"Be two bits a glass, mister—in advance."

Shiloh had traded his gold dust for greenbacks and he peeled one off his roll, then waited for his whiskey. When the glass came, he held the amber fluid up to the light, found it reasonably clear and tossed it down. Compared to the rotgut he'd swilled in the Idaho, this was pure nectar.

"Ahh," he sighed. "Bartender, bring me whatever bottle this came from."

The man nodded and brought the bottle. It was only a third full and he kept Shiloh's change.

"Say, bartender, are the poker games honest in this saloon?"

The man chuckled and wiped a few glasses with his dirty bar towel.

"Are you serious, stranger?"

"Sure."

"Then, yeah, they're honest," the bartender said with a shake of his head as he walked off to serve another customer.

"Somehow," Shiloh said to the cowboy standing next to him, "I got the impression he wasn't telling me the whole untarnished truth."

The cowboy said, "There ain't *no* poker game in this town that's honest. Ain't no law here except the law of the six-gun. Speakin' of which, I see that you wear two."

"I do."

"A man who wears two guns ought to be able to use them both, otherwise it's all just show and someone is liable to call him out into the street."

"Are you that someone?" Shiloh asked very quietly.

The cowboy studied Shiloh for a moment, then shook his head. "Nope," he said. "I pack a six-gun and the orneriest thing I ever killed with it was wearin' horns. I want no gun trouble from any man. I was just makin' idle talk."

"Idle talk like that can get a man shot," Shiloh said with a disarming grin. "You need to watch what you say or someone might take offense."

The cowboy picked up his drink and moved off down the bar, leaving Shiloh to drink alone and study the two poker games that were in progress. One was penny-ante and unworthy of Shiloh's interest, but the other had some pretty fair stakes on the table. But there wasn't room for another player.

That was just fine. Shiloh was in no hurry because it was always a good idea to size up a game for an hour or two before joining in. That way a man could see just how the deck was stacked against him. And finding that much out, he might decide to keep his money. But Shiloh was feeling reckless and that meant that, rigged or not, he would probably jump right into this game once a chair became empty.

"Excuse me," he said to the man on his right elbow.

The cowboy turned, eyed Shiloh and said, "What do you want?"

"Those boys playing poker at this near table, by chance do they ride for the Lazy B ranch?"

"Every last one of them does."

"What about that big man with the tall stack of chips and the lucky streak?"

"Why, that's Ty Ballock. It's his father, old Horatio, that built the Lazy B. Ty will inherit the whole sheebang one day."

Shiloh nodded. He could see that Ty stood out from the working cowboys. He was big, loud and profane. He also had a bad habit of dealing from the bottom of the deck.

"Anyone ever call him a cheat?" Shiloh asked with a friendly grin.

"Once. That man paid for his stupidity with a bullet in the brain. You feelin' stupid tonight, stranger?"

"Nope," Shiloh said, "but I like to win at cards just about as much as the next man."

The cowboy leaned a little closer. "I can say this because I work for another ranch—if I was you, I'd find another saloon and another card game. Ty Ballock don't like to lose, especially to strangers."

"In that case," Shiloh said, "I just might have to ruin his evening."

The cowboy looked at Shiloh as if he were crazy. "All right," he said, edging away, "just remember I warned you."

"Much obliged," Shiloh said, raising his glass of whiskey and settling in to watch the game and wait his turn.

4

IT WAS AN hour before one of the cowboys tossed in his hand and headed back to the bar to drown his losses.

Shiloh sauntered over to the game and thumbed back his Stetson. "Mind if I sit in a few hands?"

The cowboys looked to Ty Ballock, who sized Shiloh up and down as he might a horse he was thinking of buying. "I guess your money is as good as anybody's," the big man said. "But the ante is a dollar."

"That'll be just fine," Shiloh said, taking the chair and buying thirty dollars' worth of chips.

"Hope you got more money than that," Ballock said, "or you ain't going to have the pleasure of our company for very long."

"There's more if I need it," Shiloh replied, tossing in his ante along with the other cowboys.

Shiloh played conservatively for the first few hands. He lost his ante and a few dollars more, but that was the dues a man expected to pay to earn the feel of a poker game. But after about a half hour of losing, Shiloh had a pretty decent hand with three jacks. He decided it was time to see if Ballock was going to let him win a few pots or if the big rancher had it in his mind to clean his plow without winning even one hand.

"The bet is five dollars," Ballock said, studying Shiloh.

"All right. Five dollars and I'll raise it three more," Shiloh said, tossing in his money.

Everyone looked to the rancher. Ty Ballock frowned at his cards. Shiloh had realized by now he could tell by the man's expression whether he had a good hand. This time, Ballock did not. Ordinarily, a man would fold and try his luck on the next hand, but the arrogant rancher was the kind who had to look big in the eyes of a stranger right from the start.

"Well, then, I'll just raise you another ten dollars," Ballock said, grinning wickedly.

Shiloh had expected the move. He surprised everyone by meeting the raise and adding, "And I'll raise that another ten dollars."

Ballock was not pleased. "So," he growled to his cowboys, "this two-bit drifter or gunsharp thinks he's going to make himself a killin' on this hand. Well, I think he's bluffing."

Ballock slowly reached for his chips, but he didn't pick them up.

"Did you hear me, stranger?"

"Yep, I sure did," Shiloh said with an easy grin. "You said that I was a two-bit stranger who was bluffing. But you can see from my money that I'm worth more than two bits. So . . . I think you had better either put your chips in the pot and call my bluff, or fold and try to win it all back later."

Ballock was stuck. He could either look like a fool and lose a pot worth roughly a hundred dollars, or he could fold and swallow a smaller humiliation. But either way, Shiloh had the winning hand and they both knew it.

Ballock's left arm dropped to his lap, and in that instant Shiloh knew the man was extracting a card from up his sleeve.

"Put your hand back on the table where I can see it," Shiloh said in a low but very clear tone of voice.

"What!"

"I said keep your hands in plain sight."

Ballock was hunting for a reason to fight rather than lose the pot, and now he seized Shiloh's demand like a cat jumping a mouse.

"I guess," Ballock announced to everyone in the saloon as he pushed back from his chair and stood up, "that I've just been accused of cheating."

Shiloh also came to his feet. "I accused you of nothing," he said. "I just asked you to keep your hands on the table. It's not an unreasonable request. In fact, it's pretty damn well accepted that when you play cards you keep both hands in sight."

Ballock wasn't listening. "Did you boys hear the stranger? He as much as called me a cheat."

"That's right," one of the cowboys who looked a little slicker than the others said, hand dropping to shade his gun. "He as much as called you a cheat, Ty."

The big rancher turned to Shiloh with a gloating look in his eyes. "Looks like you owe me an apology."

"The hell I do."

"Get down on your knees and beg—or die," Ballock said. "The choice is yours."

"It's not a choice I admire," Shiloh said. "In fact, I think I'll turn it back around. You do the begging."

"What!" Ballock was astonished.

"You heard me," Shiloh said in a low, deadly tone of voice. "Either turn over them cards and show me what you got, or beg. Either way, the pot is mine."

Ballock looked to the one man at his table who had stood and shaded his gun. "Beeson, why don't you and me kill this sonofabitch and go find a couple of women for the night."

Beeson dipped his chin once, eyes never leaving Shiloh's face. "As long as you're payin', boss."

"I ain't payin'," Ballock said. "This dead stranger is the one that'll be payin'! Take him!"

Beeson's hand dropped for his gun but Shiloh was already slamming the poker table forward, knocking its edge into Beeson's hand and ruining his fast draw. In the instant it took for the gunslinger to recover, Shiloh's own six-gun was up and bucking in his fist. Beeson took three bullets in the chest and dropped as if pole-axed. His chin struck the edge of the table so hard they all heard a bone in his neck snap.

Shiloh swiveled the barrel of his gun and leveled it on Ty Ballock, whose own gun still hadn't cleared his holster.

"If it clears leather," Shiloh said, "you'll be pushing up daisies next spring. Choice is yours. Either get down on your knees and beg for your worthless life, or die. Which is it going to be?"

Ballock stared at the gun barrel in Shiloh's fist. He licked his lips nervously and then his eyes flicked to his men. "Take him!"

Their eyes flicked from Shiloh back to their boss. One of them stammered, "But . . . boss!"

"If you go for your guns, I'll kill him first," Shiloh said, looking right through Ballock, "and then I'll kill at least two of you before you can drag iron and gun me down."

Ballock finally understood that Shiloh wasn't a man who bluffed. "Hold it steady," he said to his men. "Maybe we just had a little misunderstanding here."

Shiloh nodded. "That's right! Your hired gun died over it and now, if you don't go down on your knees, you're going to die too. Is it real clear that I'm giving you the same choice you were going to give me?"

Ballock's face paled. "I ain't beggin' for no man!"

Shiloh cocked back the hammer of his six-gun. "One last time—on your knees or you'll die standing. Your choice, Mr. Ballock."

VENGEANCE TRAIL

"You sonofabitch!" the man wailed, sinking to his knees. "I'll see *you* beg for hell!"

"Beg!"

"I'm sorry!"

"More!" Shiloh demanded. "I want you to unbutton your sleeves and pull out the aces and other cards you're hiding!"

Ballock's face contorted with fear and rage. "Damn you!"

"Open those sleeves!"

Ballock had no choice. He unbuttoned his sleeves and cards tumbled to the floor.

Shiloh looked at the Lazy B cowboys with contempt. "How can you work for a man who cheats his own cowhands of their poor wages?"

Not one of them would answer, but Shiloh hadn't really expected they would. He stepped around the table and removed Ty Ballock's gun from its holster. "You can go now," he said, "though you could use some more practice learning how to beg."

Ballock stood up. He could not meet Shiloh's eyes, but when he spoke his voice shook with hatred. "You are a dead man! I swear on my mother's grave that I will see you grovel for mercy and then beg for death."

"Get out of here," Shiloh warned, stepping in behind the man and kicking him in the butt to propel him toward the door. "You don't deserve to live. Count yourself lucky I'm a tolerant man."

"You're a *dead* man!" Ballock shouted as he charged out of the saloon.

A moment later, a fusillade of gunfire erupted from the street and the front windows of the Delta Saloon exploded inward, shattering glass and sending everyone diving to the floor.

"Damn you!" the bartender shouted a moment later. "You get the hell out of this saloon and never come back!"

Shiloh was the only man standing. He walked over to the poker table and gathered up the chips and the money into his Stetson, then carried them to the bar.

"Cash the chips," he ordered sternly.

The bartender had a shotgun leaning up against the back bar and he gazed longingly at it, his thoughts very clear.

"It would be a real fatal decision," Shiloh said softly. "Just cash in the chips and I won't come back."

"You damn sure won't!" the bartender said. "Ty Ballock called it right—you're a dead man and I for one will spit on your grave!"

"Cash in the chips," Shiloh repeated, "before I really decide to get mad and mess up this den of thieves."

The bartender didn't have to be told a third time. He knew that Shiloh was not a man who ran a bluff. So he cashed in the chips and stood frozen, longing to grab his shotgun and blow Shiloh's back open as he moved toward the door, shattered glass crunching under his boot heels.

"You won't last two days in Chili Gulch, mister! Ballock and his men will feed what's left of you to the wolves!"

Shiloh carried his money back to the Ambassador Hotel, across the lobby filled with staring men and to the stair landing.

"Hey!" one of them yelled from over by the stove. "Did you win anything at cards!"

"Sure did," Shiloh said happily. "But you're right about the poor quality of men who drink and play cards over there—they're a hard, dishonest bunch and I don't guess I'll be keeping company with them again."

The men around the stove exchanged curious glances and watched as Shiloh went up the stairs to his room.

"Strange bastard, isn't he?" a man opined loudly.

"Yeah," another man drawled, "but at least he's interesting."

At the top of the stairs Shiloh chuckled, for he had heard those remarks and found them amusing. He had been called many things in his time, but rarely interesting.

Once back in his room, Shiloh emptied his money out on the bed and counted it twice. He had won more than a hundred dollars and that, with what he still had remaining

VENGEANCE TRAIL 35

from the sale of the Lazy B horses, gave him exactly $132.24. It wasn't a fortune, but it was enough to get him to Reno, where he could visit a real marshal's office and there, perhaps, locate an interesting Wanted poster that offered a bountiful reward.

At any rate, it was very clear to Shiloh that he would be insane to stay in Chili Gulch and wait until the Lazy B men returned in full force. With this decision made, Shiloh quickly packed his things and pulled on his old army coat, then his gloves. His intention was to go out the window and make his way down the back alley, then get to his horse and slip out of town before anyone was the wiser. Ty Ballock would not wait long to avenge his humiliation. Maybe not even until tomorrow morning.

Shiloh opened the window and a solid blast of freezing air and snow slammed into him. The blizzard was now raging at gale force and he cussed, knowing that he would probably get lost and freeze to death this night if he tried to escape town.

What to do? Shiloh slammed his widow down and rolled a smoke. He lit up and began to pace back and forth. One thing that stood to reason was that if he couldn't leave Chili Gulch, Ty Ballock couldn't leave Chili Gulch either. Right now, the humiliated rancher and his crew were probably holed up in the Bonanza Hotel just down the street.

What the hell, Shiloh thought. In the morning he'd see how hard the wind and snow were blowing. If it was possible, he could still go out his window and sneak around to his horse. He could be ten miles out of town before anyone realized he was gone.

With this in mind, Shiloh locked his door securely and prepared to sleep. He was tired and he'd stayed out too late to get his evening bath. For that matter, he hadn't even had his dinner.

But hell fire, he'd won a pot of money and he'd taken that big sonofabitch Ty Ballock down a notch or two. He'd shown the man up for what he really was—a common card cheat and not even a very good one.

Shiloh hoped the damn blizzard wore itself out by morning, because he knew he'd certainly worn out his welcome in Chili Gulch.

5

HE HAD SLEPT fitfully and was awake long before daylight, restlessly prowling back and forth in his hotel room. Just before dawn, Shiloh opened his window and stared up at the stars. To the east he could see the pale line of approaching dawn. Below him, the main street of Chili Gulch was a smooth, unviolated strip of fresh snow. As far as Shiloh could see in all directions, snow covered the sage and rocky hills.

It was time to leave this hard-luck town. Shiloh gathered up his saddlebags and the scattergun, checked his sidearms and then put a boot through the open window. The sloping roof was icy and very slick so he dropped to his hands and knees and angled toward a drain pipe that was fastened to the side wall of the Ambassador Hotel. When he reached the pipe his finger stuck to the frozen metal, and he jerked it away, leaving skin. Taking out his gloves, he put them on and gripped the pipe, then edged out over the roof and prepared to descend.

Ordinarily, he could have hugged the pipe and inched his way down, but since it had sweated and froze, it was as slick as an icicle. Shiloh dropped like a rock, and he might have broken his ankles on impact had the ground not been covered by several feet of snow.

Shiloh cussed and then stood up, brushing the snow off of himself. Taking a deep breath, he headed toward the back alley and angled toward the livery, where he would find Isaac and his sorrel gelding. He still had nearly a week's free board coming for himself and the horse, but it was time to leave Chili Gulch while he was still in good health. Last night he'd gotten the drop on Ty Ballock; there was no guarantee he'd be that lucky a second time.

Shiloh eased around behind the livery. It was possible, he reasoned, that Ballock knew that his horse was boarded there. By now he might even have learned that Shiloh had brought in three extra Lazy B horses, which Isaac had bought and then sent north on the night of Shiloh's arrival.

At any rate, Shiloh had not lived so long as a bounty hunter by taking unnecessary chances. Stepping up to the rear door of the livery, he used his teeth to remove his gloves. He put the gloves in his coat pocket and gazed eastward. The sun had detached itself from the earth and was a red ball hanging just over the horizon. It shone without warmth, but the skies were relatively clear and, with luck and without Lazy B interference, Shiloh was very hopeful that he could get to Tuscorora before nightfall.

Pushing the barn door open, Shiloh peered into the dim, musty interior. He neither saw nor heard anything, so he stepped inside with his gun clenched in his fist. He moved silently across the barn's dirt floor. When he reached the stall where his horse should have been waiting, he saw nothing—at first. But then, something made him look down onto the floor of the dark stall, and that's when he realized the sorrel was lying there and that it wasn't breathing.

Sonofabitch! he thought, opening the stall door and kneeling beside the animal. It was too dark to see anything, so he risked striking a match, and immediately he wished he hadn't. The sorrel's throat had been slit and the gelding now stared up at Shiloh with one big glazed and accusing eyeball.

"Ballock!" Shiloh spat with a murderous anger. He stood up, shaking out the match and feeling his insides churn with fury. He spun around on his heel and blindly marched across the interior of the barn until he came to a little room where he knew that Isaac slept.

"Isaac!"

There was no answer. "Isaac, wake up!"

Still no answer. Shiloh felt the hair began to rise on the back of his neck. He didn't want to light a match, but he really had no choice. The match scratched very loudly and then the small room was bathed in a sickly yellow light. The old liveryman was still in his bed. He was lying on his back and his eyes were wide open as he stared up at the ceiling with a bullet hole in his forehead.

"Damn!" Shiloh roared, swinging away and heading outside. "Damn!"

His overpowering impulse was to barge through the front door of the Bonanza Hotel and ferret out Ty Ballock and kill the man. But that impulse died before Shiloh had moved twenty paces into the street because it was exactly the kind of thing a hotheaded fool would do and get himself killed.

Shiloh halted in his tracks. There was no law in Chili Gulch. No one that he could report Isaac's murder to, not to mention the sick slaughter of his own poor horse. On the other hand, Shiloh knew that he had to do something. But, he'd do it smart, smart like a professional.

Shiloh could see the Bonanza Hotel up the street and knew it was likely that Lazy B gunmen were there lying in wait. The thing to do then was either to leave town and call it quits while he was still ahead, or to catch Ty Ballock by surprise and either kill him or give the man a lesson he would never forget.

Shiloh knew he should just leave Chili Gulch and put the whole damn mess behind him, but instead he returned to the barn, where he found a lantern. Moving back down the stalls, he had his choice of horses and he picked a dandy. It was a liver chestnut, flashy with a blaze on its face and one white stocking. The horse was a little spooked as Shiloh led it out of its stall, then quickly saddled and bridled it and tied his saddlebags and bedroll behind the cantle.

Shiloh mounted the chestnut, then rode it outside. The sun was well up now and the streets of Chili Gulch were just beginning to fill; merchants could be seen shoveling snow from in front of their various establishments. Shiloh liked the feel of the chestnut, and it seemed to want to run and carry him away from the danger in this frozen and inhospitable town. But if he ran now, he'd always feel that he'd let a real sonofabitch get away with murdering a damn good horse and a pretty decent liveryman.

Shiloh reined the chestnut up an alley and rode through the snow until he came to the back of the Bonanza Hotel. He studied the hanging fire escape and decided that he'd have no trouble if he stood up on his saddle and jumped a foot or two.

"Stick around, horse," he said, kicking out of his stirrups and climbing up onto the saddle. The horse wanted to walk until Shiloh dropped his reins to the snow. "Here goes," he muttered, leaping up and just managing to grab the bottom rail of the fire escape.

Below him, the chestnut snorted with fear and spun but it did not run away. Slipping and dangling, Shiloh finally managed to pull himself up on the fire escape and climb its icy rungs until he came to the rear fire escape door. Fortunately it was unlocked, and he was able to stumble into a very dim hallway.

Shiloh cussed at himself for having absolutely no idea which room he would find Ty Ballock in. For a minute, he stood with indecision, then he began to tiptoe down the hall, turning doorknobs. Most were locked. Two that opened were empty and another had a yellow-haired woman sleeping in a rumpled bed with two cowboys.

VENGEANCE TRAIL 41

When Shiloh reached the stairs leading down to the lobby, he froze as he saw a cowboy coming up to the second-floor landing. Shiloh flattened himself in the shadows and held his breath. The cowboy smelled heavily of liquor and didn't see Shiloh until it was too late. By then, Shiloh had the man by the throat pinned up against the wall.

"Where is Ty Ballock?" he hissed. "Answer me or I'll break your neck!"

The cowboy, whose eyes bugged with fear and lack of oxygen, gagged, "Room two-eleven."

"Thanks," Shiloh said, stepping back and throwing all his weight behind a crunching overhand right that knocked the cowboy senseless to the floor.

Shiloh knew he didn't have much time. If he was lucky, there might not be another Lazy B rider passing through the hallway for ten or fifteen minutes. That was all the time he'd need to settle affairs with Ty Ballock and then leave the same way he'd arrived.

Room 211 was very quiet until Shiloh threw his shoulder to the door and broke the lock. He crashed inside, then shut the door behind him. Ballock was alone and asleep. Now the big rancher groaned, "Go away, damn you!"

"Not hardly," Shiloh growled, striding over to the bed, grabbing Ballock by the front of his woolen long johns and dragging him into a sitting position.

Ballock must have tried to drown the previous night's humiliation because his eyes were bloodshot and his breath was stale with cigarettes and whiskey. Shiloh doubled up his fist and punched the man right in the middle of his bloated face.

"Owwww!" Ballock cried as his nose broke under Shiloh's fist. "Goddamn you, you broke my nose!"

Shiloh's answer was to hit the man again, this time in the mouth. He felt a clean satisfaction from seeing Ballock's lips turn to a red pulp. When Ballock tried to cover his face, Shiloh banged him in the ear.

"Get up and fight, horse killer!"

Ballock rolled out of bed. He was bigger and stronger than Shiloh but he was badly hurt and hung over. Shiloh gave the rancher no chance to recover. He swarmed over the man with both fists, delivering punishing blows. Ballock tried to grab Shiloh and wrestle him to the floor but Shiloh gave him no chance at all. He kept punching until Ballock's face was a crimson mess and then he attacked the rancher's stomach, pounding the breath out of him and bringing him to his knees.

Ballock was finished but not Shiloh. He sledged the man twice more, driving him to the floor.

"Stop, please!" Ballock choked, covering his face with his hands and curling into a ball.

Shiloh drew back a boot, wanting to kick the man's head in, but he couldn't. Instead, he drew his six-gun, placed its barrel next to the rancher's temple and said, "Want to tell me why you had my horse and old Isaac killed?"

"I didn't!"

"Right. Next thing you'll tell me is that my horse cut its own throat and Isaac shot himself."

Ballock said nothing, which probably saved his life.

"There is no law or court and I can't prove you guilty," Shiloh said, "but if I ever come across you again you better be reaching for your six-gun because that's what I'll be doing."

Shiloh stood up and walked over to the man's coat, shirt and trousers, which were hanging from the bedpost. He rummaged in Ballock's pockets until he found the rancher's fat wallet. Extracting all the cash, Shiloh said, "This is for damages."

Ballock looked at him and his face was almost unrecognizable. "I'll hunt you down, no matter where you go!"

"Is that right?" Shiloh laughed and pocketed a thick roll of Ballock's cash, then started to leave through the broken door.

Unfortunately, a Lazy B cowboy was coming down the hall, and when he saw Shiloh he bellowed a warning, then clawed for his gun. Shiloh shot the man in the leg and lunged at him, his pistol cracking the man's skull. He raced down the hallway to the end, tore open the fire escape door and looked down to see that the chestnut was missing!

"Uh-oh," he gulped, seeing two armed gunmen come running up the alley and hearing them shout, "There he is! On the fire escape!"

Shiloh ducked back inside as a swarm of bullets came flying up toward him. He crashed back into the hallway, feeling the noose begin to tighten around his neck. In about five seconds or less, he was sure that the hallway would be filled with Lazy B men hunting for his scalp.

With damn few options, Shiloh dashed into one of the empty rooms and locked the door behind him. He guessed he had earned about two or three minutes before his enemies would start searching each room and shooting the locks off those that were not opened on command.

Shiloh raced to the window. He pulled the shades, opened the window and gazed down at a narrow, dimly lit strip of snow between the hotel and its neighboring building. He could hear shouts in the hallway and also in the back alley.

"Damn!" Shiloh swore, jumping feet-first through the open window. He landed standing up, his boots driving deep into the snow. Climbing out, he dashed toward the main street hoping he could escape detection.

When Shiloh came to the main street, he saw the liver chestnut tied a few doors down. It might be bait, but he needed that horse and his own gear in the most desperate way imaginable. Shiloh raced down the boardwalk, tore his reins from the hitch rack and vaulted into the saddle.

The sound of gunfire filled his ears but Shiloh and the horse were already plowing their way through deep snow heading south. At the end of the street he reined the chestnut so that buildings were between him and the Lazy B cowboys.

Shiloh let the chestnut buck snow for another mile, and when it began to suck for air he reined the horse to a walk and checked himself out for any bullet wounds. He was untouched.

Shiloh reached into his coat pocket and drew out Ballock's roll of greenbacks. Licking his thumb, he counted the money and found, to his great delight, that he'd taken almost three hundred dollars!

"Couldn't happen to a finer fella," he said with a wide grin as he pushed on toward Tuscorora.

6

HORATIO BALLOCK WATCHED as his cowboys brought his only son home. Horatio could see that Ty had suffered a savage beating and that made him furious. To the old rancher's way of thinking, a man as big and strong as Ty ought never be whipped. Now he would be the laughingstock of northern Nevada.

Horatio stepped out onto his porch, and when the cowboys rode up to the hitch rail he glared at them. They did not dare to dismount, nor did they look at the crippled old rancher.

"Who did it?" Horatio demanded.

"It was a stranger," the foreman, whose name was Art Lee, said. "A man named Shiloh. We learned that he killed Clete and Matt out at the line camp. Nobody knows what happened to Jess."

"None of 'em was worth spit anyway," Horatio growled.

"Shiloh also gunned down Cole Beeson. Shot him over cards at the Delta Saloon."

"He outdrew Beeson?"

"Well, sir, Shiloh didn't exactly outdraw him, but he

rammed the poker table into Beeson's gunhand as he was makin' his play. Then he shot Beeson and got the drop on Ty. Made him show the hide-out cards up his sleeve."

Horatio's face became mottled with anger. He doubled up his fists and cursed wickedly for a full minute before he could regain control of himself, then said, "Get Ty up to his room and then get the boys out to checking the cattle. Because of the damned blizzard, some have probably drifted clear on down to the Humboldt River."

"What about Shiloh?"

Horatio stared at the nearly shapeless face of his worthless son. "Shiloh sounds to me as if he's done me a favor or two. Matt, Clete and Jess were thorns in my side and worth damn little except a swift kick in the ass. Beeson's job was to protect my boy and it's obvious that he failed. Good riddance to all of them."

"But . . ." Lee's protest died, and he swallowed and said, "Whatever you say, Mr. Ballock."

"I say we can take care of Shiloh later. I say that right now we've got cattle scattered all over the range, and half of them are probably frozen and the other half are starvin'. I want every cowboy on the payroll to get out there and take care of my herd."

"Yes, sir!"

It took four cowboys to haul Ty off his horse and carry him to his bedroom. When that was done, Horatio motioned his foreman aside. "Did you see what happened in the Delta?"

"No, sir. I was . . . well, I was with one of the girls."

"What did you hear about this man responsible for beating my son's face to pulp?"

"Nobody knows much about him," Lee said. "We found out he sold Matt's, Jess's and Clete's horse to old Isaac."

"Sold *my* horses!"

"Yes, sir. Old Isaac musta figured he could sneak 'em on up into Idaho and resell 'em for a pretty good profit."

"That sneaky little sonofabitch!" Horatio raged. "He

knows better than to try and double-cross me!"

"Well, sir, he ain't ever going to do it again."

Horatio's bushy eyebrows lifted in question. "What did you do to him?"

"Ty shot him in his bed, sir. Shot him right between the eyes. He also . . ."

"Also what? Don't hold a thing back on me, Art! You know I'll find out everything anyway."

The foreman shifted uncomfortably. "Well, sir, I wasn't in on that either. And I know you won't approve, but Ty slit the stranger's horse from ear to ear."

"Jaysus!" Horatio bellowed. "Ty knows I won't abide killin' good saddle horses! What Ty should have done is to steal the man's horse and maybe lure him out here where we could have some fun before killin' him."

"Yes, sir, I'm sure that Ty realizes that he made a bad mistake. I guess that's why Shiloh came lookin' for Ty early this morning and caught him hung over and asleep in bed. Musta beat him up before Ty could even climb to his feet and defend himself. Ty's too big and strong to be whipped by any ordinary-sized man."

"And Shiloh is ordinary sized?"

"Maybe a little taller and heavier than average. 'Bout two hundred pounds but no more. Maybe six feet tall but real strong and tough looking."

"Tough?" Horatio barked a laugh. "We'll see how tough he is when I get ahold of him. Is he fast on the draw?"

"Damn fast."

Horatio scrubbed at the stubble on his beard. "Which way did he ride out of Chili Gulch?"

"South, toward Tuscorora."

"Do you think he's a gunfighter?"

Lee thought about that for several minutes before he shook his head. "Sir, I just don't know. My gut feeling is that Shiloh isn't a hired gun, but he is definitely one mean sonofabitch."

Horatio nodded. "When the cattle are rounded up and

these damn freak blizzards blow over, I want you to take four or five or however many men you think you'll need and go find Shiloh. Bring him back alive if you can."

"And if we can't?"

"Kill him any way that you can. If we let this thing pass, I'll lose respect. Once that happens, it's over."

"Yes, sir." The foreman turned to leave. Art Lee was not a young man, and he had worked for the Lazy B for more than twenty years before being made foreman.

"Oh, and Art?"

He turned to face Horatio. "Sir?"

"Next time you aren't around to keep Ty out of harm's way, I'll have you tied wrists to ankles over a hitch rail. I'll have your pants pulled down and then I'll peel the hide off your ass with my old bullwhip. Do you understand me?"

Art Lee's cheeks drained of color and he nodded. He feared Ty because the man was strong and mean, but he feared old Horatio even more because he was cunning and totally ruthless.

"Yes, sir!"

"Get the hell out of my sight," Horatio growled before he turned and hobbled into the house. He went to his son's bedroom and closed the door.

"Are you gonna tell me about it now or later?" the rancher demanded, even as he judged he'd never seen a more terrible beating.

Ty attempted to see his father, even though his eyes were both nearly swollen shut. "Pa," he choked, "can't you see I'm hurt!"

"You big, dumb bastard! Why didn't you kill Shiloh along with his horse and Isaac?"

"Tried to, Pa! Thought he'd come to us, rather than the other way around."

"So you got drunk the night before and Shiloh caught you off guard! Is that it?"

Ty peered through the slits of his swollen lids. "Sir, I never thought—"

VENGEANCE TRAIL 49

"You never think period!" Horatio raged. "That part you get from your mother. She was just a common whore and I never should have taken and raised you for my son. You're stupid and a fool! When I die, you won't get this spread. You couldn't run it for a month without losing it."

Horatio turned away with a growl of disgust. He stomped to the door and turned. "Ty, I've made up my mind—when you heal, I'm sending you packin'."

"Pa!"

"I mean it! You're worthless and you always will be."

"But you can't do that!"

"Oh, can't I?" Horatio asked. "Just wait and see what I can or cannot do. You're finished on the Lazy B. When I die, I'll pass the ranch on to someone that I know who can at least keep it together."

"Someone like Art Lee!" Ty choked. "That ass-kisser!"

"Maybe he is," Horatio said, "but at least he's not a complete fool. With him in charge of the Lazy B, I'll rest in peace."

"You're gonna rest in hell!" Ty shouted as his father slammed the door and stomped down the hallway.

For the next four hours, Ty lay flat on his back awash in a sea of pain and fear. He'd never seen his father so angry, and the thought of being disinherited made him sick to his stomach.

What would he do without this ranch? He sure as hell wasn't skillful enough with a rope or on a horse to make his living cowboying. He'd never had to do hard physical work because there were always men like Art Lee and the others to do it for him.

"I can't let Pa do this," Ty muttered. "I've got to make him change his mind!"

How? That was the question that burned in Ty's fevered mind. One way would be for Ty to show his father once and for all that he could handle his own troubles. And right now, his number-one trouble was the man called Shiloh.

Ty pushed himself to his feet. He staggered over to the

mirror and a moan escaped his lips when he saw what Shiloh had done to his poor face. He would never look the same.

"I'll find and kill him if it's the last thing I ever do!" he breathed.

Ty stumbled back to his bed and floated away in a haze of red misery. He would, of course, need a little help to kill Shiloh, and that would take money—lots of money. Fortunately, Ty had some money stashed away. Enough to hire one of the fastest guns in Nevada, a man who lived in a nearby town called North Fork and who was known in this part of the country as Falcon. Falcon was a backshooter first, a gunfighter second and knife-fighter third. He was the most dangerous man Ty had ever seen and one of the few that he really feared.

Yes, Ty thought, Falcon and me will find this Shiloh fella and settle the score. And when I bring Shiloh's head back here in a canvas bag, Pa will realize I'm a better man than that ass-kisser Art Lee.

7

TUSCORORA WAS FAR more to Shiloh's liking than Chili Gulch. It was about three times bigger, and for a man with money to spend, a good time could be had in Tuscorora. The town's economy was fed by a number of big mines that dotted the neighboring hills. Mines like the Grand Prize and the Northern Belle. There were also several mills at the edge of town, where the ore was smelted using tons of sagebrush cut by an army of Chinese who had lost their jobs after the completion of the transcontinental railroad. The Chinese were the only men willing to drag their handcarts out into the sage hills. There, day after day they hacked away the tough and tick-infested brush, which they sold to the smelters for two dollars a cord, cut, smashed down flat and delivered.

Off in the distance, the Independence Mountains stood in a violet haze against the blue sky. Big cattle ranches operated in their foothills, where streams provided a year-round source of water and grass. And in the town itself, there was good whiskey and pretty women to be had for a fair price.

Shiloh stayed at the Overland Hotel on Weed Street, and

he ate well at the many good cafés that dotted the main street. But always he kept his eyes open for trouble coming from the direction of Chili Gulch.

"It's coming," he told himself each morning as he dressed in front of his mirror, then patted his guns and holsters before going down the stairs to breakfast.

Some men might have wondered why Shiloh didn't clear out of the territory, and his answer would have been that he'd learned from his experiences as a bounty hunter that a man could run but he could not hide. Not even in the vast, empty expanses of the American West. Besides, who in his right mind wanted to live always looking over his shoulder? No sir! To Shiloh's way of thinking, a man who ran from trouble was a man who lived with the beast of fear eating up his insides.

"What'll it be this morning, Shiloh?" a fat but friendly waitress asked as he took his place at the café counter and studied the menu written up on a chalkboard. There was always the same three choices all times of the day: steak and fried potatoes, pork and fried potatoes, or mutton and fried potatoes.

"When is someone around here going to raise a few chickens?" Shiloh groused. "I'd pay a dollar for a damned egg."

"It'd cost us that much just to serve them," the woman, whose name was Josie, said cheerfully. "You see, we'd have to send all the way to California for layin' hens. Now, if they didn't die on the way across this desert, they'd sure enough be killed by coyotes."

"You could build a chicken house once they arrived."

"Then thieves would steal and butcher them instead of losin' 'em to the coyotes."

"How do you know that?"

"Because."

"Because of what?" Shiloh asked with exasperation.

"Listen," she said, "the boss bought a whole mess of quail chicks last year from the Paiute Indians. Musta been a hundred or more of those chirpin' little shitters. Anyway, we built a little house out back and we planned to raise the damned things and sell their eggs. But you know what?"

Shiloh could guess but he said nothing.

"Well, sir, someone stole every damn one of them quail the minute they was full growed!"

"You ever find out who did it?"

"No, but the boss said he heard they was servin' roast quail at the Townhouse Café. He went over there and demanded to see the quail 'cause he knew they were ours."

"What happened?"

Josie threw up her hands in a gesture of futility. "The owner of the café claimed he'd bought quail from the Paiutes too! Said it was different quail and that, since you couldn't brand the little bastards, my boss had no legal claim."

"I think he had a good point," Shiloh conceded.

"Sure he did! The boss was so mad he couldn't see straight for nearly a week. He'd become real attached to those quail and claimed he knew every individual in the flock and had even named most of them. For about a month, he swore he was going to go back to the Townhouse Café and, if he didn't get them quail back, he was going to blow them all to hell with buckshot! That way, nobody could have them."

"Did he?"

"Naw." Josie laughed. "Someone stole them again! Probably the same fella that stole them from us. My guess is that them same quail are probably makin' the rounds of cafés all over this part of Nevada."

"How interesting," Shiloh deadpanned.

"So," Josie said, "what'll it be?"

"Oh, I think I'll have beef and potatoes."

"That's what you have *every* morning."

"I know."

Josie shook her head. "I don't even know why I bother to ask you, Shiloh."

"Then don't," he said with a wink.

Shiloh enjoyed the café very much. With money to spend, he tipped Josie almost as much as the price of his meal, and in return he got the best service along with about five refills of coffee.

After breakfast Shiloh went outside and strolled down to the saddle shop where he had his eye on a new bridle and pair of fancy reins for the liver chestnut. The bridle and reins were made out of latigo leather and were beautifully stitched with two shiny silver conchos. The saddlemaker, a Mexican named José Escobar, also had a few saddles for sale. One in particular appealed to Shiloh because of its excellent silver work and leather carving.

"You should buy it!" Escobar said, flashing a gold tooth and a wide grin. "Every day you come in and look at that saddle like a child looking at a toy. If you want it so bad, amigo, maybe I could drop the price a little."

The saddle was seventy dollars. Most cowboys paid twenty-five or thirty for a rough working saddle, but this one was much more expensive because of the silver and fancy tooling.

"Naw," Shiloh said.

"What if I gave it to you for . . . sixty dollars?"

"Nope."

"No?" Escobar looked insulted. "Then what about fifty dollars? Come on, amigo! My seven children need to eat!"

Shiloh chuckled. He'd seen Escobar's children and they were all as chubby as chipmunks. "Afraid not."

"Then what would you pay for that saddle, señor?"

"I *can't* buy it," Shiloh admitted.

"But I hear you have much dinero!"

"I have the money," Shiloh said, "but in my line of business, a man doesn't want to wear things that shine in the sunlight. The men I hunt would like to see the warning glint of that beautiful silver very much, comprende?"

"Sí," the Mexican said with a reluctant nod of his head.

"But maybe you should buy this saddle and then take up another line of work?"

"Such as?"

Escobar shrugged his round shoulders. "Maybe become a sheriff. Tuscorora could use a good sheriff."

"Probably," Shiloh said, "but telling folks to behave and obey the law isn't something I'd enjoy."

"So," Escobar said, "maybe you enjoy hunting men like I hunt rabbits?"

"No," Shiloh said, replacing the bridle and reins, "but my line of work is very interesting. Especially when you go after a seasoned outlaw. One that realizes he's got a hunter on his trail and knows how to make his tracks disappear. Either that, or one that has the guts to set a clever ambush."

Escobar's smile died as he listened. "I think maybe I am glad to be making saddles and bridles instead of hunting desperados, eh, señor?"

"Someone has to do it when the law can't," Shiloh said, heading for the door. "And the ones that do it best can make good money."

"You earn it, señor," the Mexican said with a nod of his chins. "As for me, the only thing I hunt is tequila in a town that thirsts only for beer or whiskey."

Shiloh chuckled sympathetically then went outside. It had not snowed for a week and the weather was finally starting to warm up. He thought it was about time to ride for the Comstock Lode or Reno. And yet, he was still in need of rest, and since he was enjoying himself in Tuscorora he figured he'd stay a few more days.

Besides, he had found himself a good poker game every night, and while he hadn't made a killing, he was steadily adding to his winnings. Right now he had almost four hundred dollars to his name, and had set his mind on getting five hundred before he saddled the chestnut and rode west.

He was thinking about all this when he saw two men

round the corner and ride slowly up the street. One was big and thick, with bull shoulders and a floppy hat pulled down to his eyebrows, leaving his face in shadow. The other man was thin and hatchet-faced with a wispy blond mustache. He was wearing a fancy black leather jacket and a white Stetson. His pants were tucked into the tops of a pair of tan boots and his spurs were silver.

The smaller one was a dandy, but Shiloh was more interested in the big man because somehow he was very familiar. The pair reined up and dismounted at the end of Weed Street, then talked for a minute and separated. The big man took the dandy's horse and left him on the boardwalk.

It was strange to Shiloh how, after years of hunting men, he had developed a sort of sixth sense about danger, and as the dandy came sauntering up the street, Shiloh felt danger. But why? Who was this man and who was his huge companion? And almost as he asked this question, Shiloh knew the answer. The big man was Ty Ballock. As for the dandy, chances were he would be a hired gunfighter.

Shiloh ducked into a saloon. Without a word, he passed on through and out the back door into the alley. Taking the alley at a run, he hurried in the direction he'd seen Ty Ballock moving. Shiloh figured if he was going to have to defend himself, he would much prefer to individually face the man who wanted his hide.

When Shiloh burst out of the alley, he saw that Ballock had reached a livery. The big man was handing the reins of both horses to a livery boy when he realized that Shiloh was coming at him from across the street.

Ballock's face was still a mess and covered with deep purple blotches. His nose was twisted and his lips were puffy. There was an ugly scar on his cheek, all compliments of Shiloh's fists.

Shiloh's hands were near his guns and he expected the big man to draw. Instead, Ballock grabbed the livery boy and dropped to one knee as he drew his six-gun and pressed it to the boy's head.

"I'll kill him!" Ballock shouted. "You come any closer and I'll kill him!"

The boy struggled like a rabbit caught in a trap but he was helpless in Ballock's grasp.

"Let him go!" Shiloh bellowed. "He's no part of this!"

But the rancher wasn't about to let his shield go. Instead, he dragged the boy forward, taking aim at Shiloh, who began to backpedal as he drew his own guns. "Let him go!"

In reply, Ballock unleashed two shots and Shiloh heard the second one whistle past his ear. He wanted, in the worst way, to open fire, but he was afraid of killing the boy. That being the case, and with Ballock drawing steadily nearer, Shiloh had no choice but to turn on his heels and run.

He could hear the boy screaming in fright, but he could also hear Ballock's hyena laughter, and that was most galling of all. Shiloh felt the sting of a bullet enter the flesh of his right buttock just before he threw himself around a building and out of Ballock's sights. He slapped his hand back, and when he brought it up before his eyes it was smeared with blood.

Shiloh ran back up the alley, feeling the fire in his butt turn to a dull ache. He was probably bleeding heavily and, if he lived through this day, he'd be willing to bet that he'd not comfortably sit that horse of his for many a day.

Shiloh dashed through the saloon again and this time stopped long enough to buy a shot of whiskey. Turning his backside to the bar, he yelled, "Douse me!"

"What!" the bartender asked in a shocked voice.

"Douse my ass!"

"Well you can *kiss* my ass, mister! I sell *drinking*' whiskey."

Shiloh cussed and took the shot glass, then doused his own behind. The liquor made the wound sting like fiery nettles. "How bad does it look?" he asked a drunken cowboy who was staring stupidly at the wound.

"Looks nasty, mister," the cowboy drawled. "Damn nasty. Almost makes a fella want to puke!"

"Dammit!" Shiloh swore, heading on through the bar. "Bunch of weak-bellied sonsabitches!"

He stepped out with a gun in his fist, eyes frantically searching for either Ty Ballock or the rancher's professional gunfighter. Seeing neither man, Shiloh hobbled up the street, one hand holding his poor torn cheek, the other wrapped around his six-gun.

Shilo ducked into the hotel where he was staying and limped painfully over to the startled desk clerk. "Send a doctor up to my room right now," he ordered.

The clerk just stared.

"Didn't you hear me!"

"Yes, sir!"

"Good! Then do it!" Shiloh shouted, heading for his room.

Inside, he quickly pulled down his pants and found a handkerchief to staunch the bleeding. What miserable luck this was! And now he had two men hunting for him and one of them was a professional.

Shiloh was not pleased. He was not all that worried about Ty Ballock in a one-to-one fight. Ballock was strong, but like many heavily muscled men, rather slow. But the little gunfighter?

Shiloh checked to make sure that his room was bolted and then he flopped stomach-first down on his bed. Hatchet-Face was going to be a real worry until one or the other of them were dead.

8

WHEN THE KNOCK sounded on Shiloh's door, he rolled off the bed and padded softly over to the door. "Who is it?"

"It's Doc Weaver. Do you need medical attention in there?"

"Afraid so," Shiloh grunted, unlocking the door and opening it to see a silver-haired man with a battered medical kit.

"What's wrong with you?" the doctor asked. "You look fine."

Shiloh did an about-face. "You still think so?"

"Shot you in the butt, huh?"

"That's right. I don't know if the bullet is still in there or not."

"Why don't you drop your drawers and then get over on the bed and let's have a look."

Shiloh nodded. He locked the door, causing the doctor to give him a curious look. Shiloh explained, "It's for both our protections."

"Someone comin' to shoot you again?"

"I expect they'll want to try," Shiloh said. "But that's none of your concern, Doc. Let's get this over with."

The doctor was not a bit happy about the situation. "Listen, young fella. I got a sickly wife and I don't need any trouble. I'm this town's only real doctor and people would be damned upset if I was to get caught in some feud that you might have goin' on."

"Doc," Shiloh said with impatience, "the sooner you start fixin' instead of talkin', the sooner you can get out of here and leave me to my own misery."

Doc Weaver wasn't happy but he could see that Shiloh was not about to let him turn and go away. "All right, drop them."

Shiloh dropped his pants and felt the doctor's cold hands on his cheeks. "Ouch!" he yelped. "Doc, that's not a loaf of bread you're squeezin' so hard!"

"Shut up and don't move!"

Shiloh ground his teeth until the doctor finished his examination. He had rougher hands than a goddamn blacksmith.

"Well," the doc said at last, "I need to dig a bullet out. You'll have to come to my office."

"No!"

"What do you mean, 'no'? Of course you will! That bullet is in there someplace and it'll fester until half your ass falls away. We've got to dig it out."

"I understand," Shiloh said, "but you're going to do it here and you're going to do it now."

The doctor's eyes widened. "The hell with that! I didn't even bring my chloroform."

"Never mind the chloroform," Shiloh snapped. "I can't afford to be helpless in case they barge in during the operation."

"Who?" The doctor whirled toward the door. "Mister, I'm getting out of here!"

Shiloh stood to grab the doctor before he could reach the door. Unfortunately, Shiloh's pants were down around his ankles and they tripped him. He fell but managed to get his hands on the doctor's leg and drag him to the floor. The old bird put up quite a struggle but he was no match for Shiloh.

"All right," Shiloh said, wincing with pain as he pulled his six-gun out of his holster. "I ain't got the time to wrestle around with you anymore. Now if you try and squirt out of here again, I'm going to use this gun on you."

The doctor believed him. He nodded his head up and down rapidly. "All right," he said, "but I won't be held responsible for this operation. The pain will be considerable without chloroform."

Shiloh found a pint of whiskey. He took three long slugs. "Let's get this done with."

"Okay, lie down on the bed and take a bite out of your pillow or you'll scream your damned ugly head off."

Shiloh did as he was told, but he kept his head craned around toward the door and he kept his gun ready in case Ty Ballock decided to come barreling through with his guns blazing.

Shiloh did not think he needed to bite a pillow until the doctor rammed a forcep into his buttock and started probing for the slug. From that moment on he hollered like a scalded dog, but by keeping a bite on the pillow, he managed to keep the noise down. Sweat poured from his body and he writhed on the bed, trying to keep still and yet unable to do so.

"Ain't you about got it!" he finally gasped.

"It's in there pretty deep," the doctor said, digging into his kit and finding a longer pair of forceps. "And I've got to make a wider incision in order to get these bigger forceps in deep enough."

"Damn!" Shiloh swore, biting down on the pillow again.

It seemed like an eternity before the doctor stopped digging and cutting. "There!" he cried, dragging out the bloody slug and dropping it on Shiloh's pillow. "Got the little bugger!"

Shiloh was too drained to say much. He flicked the slug away with the barrel of his gun.

"I'll pack this with sulfa powder and cotton," the doctor said. "Hopefully it will heal without too much infection. How do you feel?"

"Like a man with two assholes."

The doctor chuckled, suddenly relaxed now that the operation was successfully completed. "You've lost a fair amount of blood. There's a lot of blood vessels in the old gluteus maximus."

"The what?"

"Never mind. But you will probably feel a little weak for a day or two."

"If I live that long," Shiloh said, pushing up to his feet and indeed feeling a little lightheaded.

"Are your enemies coming for you right now?" the doctor asked, wiping his scalpel and forceps clean on the bedsheets.

"They're probably searching from one hotel to the next," Shiloh admitted.

"Why?"

"They want to kill me."

"Why?"

Shiloh sighed. "What difference does it make to you, Doc?"

The old man frowned. "Well, if you aren't a murderer, rapist or robber, then I was thinking I might offer you a place to heal and hide."

"I don't understand."

"Well, I have this little recovery place in my backyard for patients that need regular medical attention. It's just an old converted stable, but I've had it fixed up decent with a bed, stove and an outhouse outside. You can hide there and no one will find you until you're strong enough to take care of yourself."

"Now why would you do this for me, a fella who had to tackle, then hold a gun on you?"

"For money, of course. My offer doesn't come cheap."

"How much?"

VENGEANCE TRAIL 63

The doctor stroked his chin. "Oh, let's just deal in round figures. Say that my surgical services just rendered, coupled with a week in the stable-house will all total just a hundred dollars."

"A hundred dollars!"

"With meals—good ones, too," the doctor added quickly.

When Shiloh hesitated, the doctor added, "You are in no shape to defend yourself in your weakened condition. Furthermore, without regular medical attention and dressing changes, you will likely have serious problems. You jested about having a second asshole, but it might not be such a joke by next week if that wound becomes infected."

Shiloh gulped. It was apparent that Doc Weaver wasn't bluffing and the prospects of which he spoke made Shiloh shudder. "All right," he said quickly, "a hundred dollars."

"In advance. Just in case they do find and kill you before the week is out."

Shiloh could see the doctor's point of view so he didn't argue and paid the man. The doctor gave him directions. "My suggestion is to leave this hotel at once."

"In broad daylight? Doc, a man with a hole in his butt is going to attract some attention."

"True." The doctor frowned. "Oh, very well, I'll bring a buckboard and a tarp around behind this hotel in a few minutes. You can jump under the tarp and then I'll drive you right into my backyard. With any luck at all, no one will be any the wiser."

Shiloh wasn't thrilled with the plan, but since he could think of none better, he nodded his head. "Just don't double-cross me, Doc. I wouldn't like to turn a sickly wife into a sickly widow."

The doctor nodded. "I understand you very well."

"Good," Shiloh said, handing the man another ten dollars.

"What's this for?"

"Buy me a couple pair of new pants. Medium size."

"All right."

When the doctor was gone, Shiloh went to the window, where he slipped the curtains aside a crack and looked out into the street. He didn't see either Ty Ballock or the hired gun, but he knew they were out there and that they were searching like crazy men for him this very minute. Ballock would know his bullet had wounded Shiloh and the big bastard would probably be flush with revenge and the anticipation of a kill.

Well, Shiloh thought, if he could just get to the doc's little hideaway and rest up a few days until he got his blood and strength back, things might take a surprising turn for the better. One thing for sure, with his butt throbbing like a toothache and his head a little dizzy, things could not get a whole hell of a lot worse than they were right now—he hoped.

9

"THE SONOFABITCH HAS *got* to be around somewhere!" Ty ranted as he and Falcon returned to the site of the shooting nearly an hour earlier. "I know I hit him with one of my shots!"

"Where?"

"In the back, I think. Maybe in the ribs," Ty said, shrugging his big shoulders. "I don't know for sure. I just saw him stagger before he disappeared around the corner."

"Exactly where did he stagger?"

"Hell," Ty groused, "I don't know! About over there by the corner of that shack."

Falcon walked swiftly over to the place. He thumbed back his Stetson and squatted on his boot heels, eyes searching the ground until he saw a spot of blood. "Here it is," he said, standing up and following the trail into the alley. "He was bleeding pretty heavily, too."

Falcon said nothing but kept his eyes on the ground. Every yard or so there was a spattering of blood. Not a significant amount until you realized that Shiloh had been running for his life.

They followed the trail of blood spots, Ty Ballock forging impatiently ahead, Falcon shouting at the much larger man not to stomp out the trail.

"Here," Falcon whispered when they came to the rear door of a saloon. "He went in right here."

Ballock stepped aside and hissed, "He's all yours. Wound him if you can 'cause I want to finish him off slow."

Falcon did not respond because he had no intention of wounding any adversary. He was a professional and never shot except to kill. Drawing his six-gun, Falcon turned the knob and eased into the back of the saloon, gun sweeping the dim, vacant interior. Falcon then moved swiftly into the saloon itself, spotting several dark splotches of blood on the sawdust floor.

He went up to the bartender, gun still in his fist. "You see a wounded man come running through here about thirty or forty minutes ago?"

"Yeah," the bartender said nervously. "He wanted me to douse his backside with whiskey and then he ran out the front door."

"He was shot in the butt?" Falcon asked, casting a look of contempt at Ty Ballock.

"That's right."

Falcon wasn't pleased. A bullet in the side might be fatal but a bullet in the butt was just painful. "Which way did he go when he left?"

"To the right."

"You know where he's staying?"

"No. I never seen him before," the bartender said.

Falcon turned to the other patrons. "I've got five dollars for the man who can tell me where the wounded man is right now!"

A miner tossed down the dregs of his beer and stepped forward. "I happened to be comin' in when that jasper came chargin' out with a gun in one hand and a fist full of his own ass in the other. He damn near knocked me down. I yelled at him to watch himself but he didn't even hear me. I stood out there watching him run up the street and I saw where he went."

"Where?" Falcon asked.

The miner winked at his friends. "Don't you boys think that this information ought to be worth at least twenty dollars?"

The other miners and cowboys all nodded in agreement. The man turned back to Falcon. "You got twenty dollars, mister?"

Falcon's thin face never changed expression as he said, "No, but I got something else."

"What'd that be?" the miner asked with a smirk on his face.

"This," Falcon said, drawing his gun and slashing it across the miner's mouth, breaking his teeth.

The miner cried out in pain and shock. Several of the men in the saloon started to jump up but Falcon had already twisted the miner around so that he was between himself and the others and had the gun jammed into his side.

"Now," Falcon whispered, "where did you say that buttshot went to hide?"

The young miner had to choke out the words but they were still intelligible. "The Overland! The Overland Hotel!"

"Thanks," Falcon said, shoving the man away and heading out the door with Ballock hurrying after.

"Hey, you didn't pay him that five dollars!" someone yelled from the saloon they'd just left behind.

Falcon had no intention of paying anyone anything.

"You play real rough, don't you," Ballock said with admiration.

Falcon looked him right in his swollen, purplish eyes and said, "So does the man we're trying to kill."

"Right," Ballock said, looking away quickly.

As they started for the Overland Hotel, Falcon said, "Why don't you just wait in the lobby? Or better yet, go around to the back in case he tries to duck out into the alley."

"I'd rather stick with you."

"I don't give a damn what you'd rather do," the gunfighter said. "You'll do what I say."

Ballock started to argue but changed his mind. He stomped out the back way as Falcon went in the front. Ballock was furious. Furious at himself for not getting a killing shot into Shiloh, and furious because he had to take orders from Falcon, who was an insufferable bastard. Well, he thought as he marched down the narrow corridor between the hotel and a saloon, with luck Shiloh will be dead inside of the next few minutes.

"Howdy," Shiloh said quietly as he stepped out of the shadows. "What's the matter, are you lost again?"

Ty Ballock had been so angry that he'd not been paying attention to things and now, here was the man that he both feared and hated. Ballock's hand dropped to his gun and he made what he thought was a very good draw, but in the dim canyon between the two buildings he saw the double flash and heard the muffled report of Shiloh's guns, and Ballock realized he was staggering backward. He slammed up against the wall and stared down at his own gun, which he was amazed to find still resting in his holster.

Ballock felt his knees break and he began to slide down the side of a splintery plank wall. "You . . ."

"Lose," Shiloh said, finishing the man's sentence and then holstering his guns as he turned and limped away. A moment later, Shiloh met Doc Weaver in the alley and slipped under the tarp.

"You were supposed to wait behind the Overland!" the doc snapped, driving the wagon along.

"I forgot," Shiloh lied.

"Well, dammit," the doc growled, "you'd better start remembering things or we'll both be in deep trouble."

Shiloh said nothing. He figured that the hatchet-faced man would be barging into his vacated hotel room about now. He'd see the blood on the bed and he'd know that his quarry had been hit pretty solidly and had lost a good deal of blood. Maybe he'll ride out now that the man who paid him is dead, Shiloh thought hopefully.

But maybe not. A gunfighter had to honor the code of his profession, and that code was to deliver the services he was paid for. So, if Ballock had already paid, the gunfighter would not leave Tuscorora until either he or his quarry was dead.

Shiloh closed his eyes. There was no use in worrying about the gunfighter now. Shiloh needed to regain his strength while his butt wound cleanly healed. After that, if the gunfighter was still combing the town for him, they would have their little showdown and one of them would end up planted six feet under this hard, frozen ground.

In the days following the death of Ty Ballock, Falcon paced the streets of Tuscorora like a caged tiger. That first day he learned where Shiloh had boarded his horse, and he often dropped by the stable at odd hours in the hopes of catching Shiloh trying to escape. There were two stagecoaches that left town each day and Falcon was always at the station making sure that Shiloh was not on board.

But mostly, Falcon watched Doc Weaver, for he was certain that Tuscorora's only physician must have treated Shiloh's wound. Falcon watched the old doctor when he rushed out to deliver Mrs. Potter's first child, and he followed him when the doctor hurried to a mine cave-in just north of town where three men were buried alive and two were badly crushed. He saw Doc Weaver greet the sick and the elderly through his office window, and once he saw the doctor treat a drunk who had been run over by an ore wagon and had both his legs broken. But day and night, he never once saw the doctor go anywhere to visit and treat the man called Shiloh.

"He's the only link that I have," Falcon said to himself one evening as the doctor went out to his little carriage house for what Falcon had come to believe were canned fruits and vegetables kept in storage.

But this night, the doctor did not return as quickly as usual and Falcon became curious. When the doctor did finally reappear to return to his house, Falcon saw the man peer all around him into the darkness as if searching for danger. It was at that moment that Falcon knew the doctor had been hiding Shiloh all along. When he was certain that the doctor had gone to bed and when the hour grew very late, Falcon slipped across the doctor's backyard. He was slender and quick, a rather graceful man much younger looking than his thirty-four years.

Falcon waited against the little stable-house a few minutes, then drew his six-gun and edged along until he came to the door. He dropped to his knees and tried to peer under the door to see if there was any light inside. There was none. This was bad. Falcon knew that if he came charging through the doorway, he would be more visible than Shiloh, who would be impossible to see in the dark interior of the room. Falcon stood and gently leaned against the structure, forcing his mind to stop racing and methodically go over his options, which were either to go in blind or wait until daylight and then try and bust in and catch Shiloh off guard.

Falcon was naturally an impatient man, but when it came to stalking and killing a worthy adversary such as this, he had developed great patience. He decided to wait until just after daylight and then bust through the door and hope to catch Shiloh asleep in his bed. Two bullets, one in the body and the next in the brain and his job would be finished. That way, he could report to old Horatio Ballock that his son's death had been avenged. Horatio would probably reward him with a bonus. The old man was tough, but he was willing to pay for favorable results.

Falcon backtracked across the yard. Once in the alley, he returned to his own hotel room and removed his boots, coat and the little string tie he favored.

He would relax, perhaps even doze off and on through the rest of the long night, and just before dawn he'd awaken to finish the job that would not only preserve, but enhance his reputation.

Too bad about that fool Ty Ballock. But the man had always been an accident waiting to happen. He'd been slow and stupid, and while that might be fine if you were a common miner, cowboy or teamster, it would not do if you crossed bullets with a real fighting man. And from all that Falcon had heard, Shiloh was nothing if not a professional like himself.

10

SHILOH HAD NOT slept well that night. He'd suffered through another battlefield slaughter scene, and when he awoke covered with his usual cold sweat, he'd lain for hours staring into the darkness. There was another thing that worried at his mind, and that was something the doctor had told him during the previous evening.

"This gunfighter named Falcon," the doctor had confided, "he is following me. I know that he thinks that I'll lead him to you. That's why I'll be glad when you're gone."

Shiloh had sensed real fear in the doctor's voice. Not that he could blame Weaver, because anyone would feel spooked with a man like Falcon shadowing your every move. Shiloh lit a match and touched it to the wick of the candle placed near his bed. He rolled out of bed and limped to the door and made sure that it was securely bolted. Staying penned up in this tiny cubicle hadn't been easy for him. He'd played a lot of solitaire and the doctor had limited him to a pint of whiskey a day. His butt was well on the mend, but he sure wasn't up to leaving Tuscorora on horseback.

Shiloh dressed and made up his mind that he would at least go outside and take a leak, then get a little fresh air before daylight. After that, he could not risk being seen standing around in the doctor's backyard.

The night air was bracing and Shiloh filled his lungs with it and gazed up at the fading stars. He thought about the hatchet-faced man whose name he'd come to learn was Falcon. Would he be forced to kill Falcon before he could leave Tuscorora? It seemed there would be little choice since the hired gunman had not pulled stakes after finding Ty Ballock gunned down beside the Overland Hotel. In a way, that impressed Shiloh because it said that Falcon had a code of honor.

Shiloh reached back and massaged his butt. The doctor had stopped using bandages—hell, they didn't stay on worth a damn anyway. The wound had closed and stopped draining, and now it was just a matter of pain and not doing anything that would tear the wound open and create any new problems.

Shiloh filled his lungs and thought about Virginia City. He'd been thinking about going to the Comstock a lot lately. There was a big-hearted madam named Julia up there who had taken a special shine to him and the feeling was mutual. There was also a lot of money floating around and enough drunken miners to take it from over the saloon card tables. Virginia City would be starting to warm up a little and the snow would probably be about melted away just as it was starting to melt off here in Tuscorora. Shiloh pretty much decided that, if he could, he'd head west in the next day or two.

He was thinking about this and peering up at the last of the stars when he heard the dog next door suddenly begin to bark. And not just a sleepy hello or good-morning bark, either. No sir, this was an urgent bark and it caused Shiloh to jump back inside the stable-house and grab one of his six-guns. He did not close the door but stood beside it waiting. If Falcon had discovered his hiding place, well

VENGEANCE TRAIL 75

and good. It was time to dance until only one of them was left standing on the floor.

Shiloh waited until the first light of dawn was streaking across the eastern horizon, then waited still more until the night gave way to full daylight. But Falcon did not come, if indeed it had been him in the first place. Finally, Shiloh closed and bolted his door, then went back to his bed wondering what had upset the damned dog.

Falcon had not anticipated a dog's anxious barking. There had been no dog the night before to raise hell, and he supposed it must have been closed up inside or off doing whatever dogs do at night. At any rate, once the damned thing had set up a ruckus, Falcon knew that the game was up and that it would be stupid to try to catch a man as dangerous as Shiloh by surprise.

And yet, he was also unwilling to wait another twenty-four hours since to do so would be to lose an edge to his mental readiness. This being the case, Falcon made another decision and walked up to Doc Weaver's house. It was still very early and no one was up yet. Falcon banged on the front door and kept banging until he heard a sleepy voice from inside the hall. "Who the hell is it at this hour!"

Falcon stepped to one side of the door and groaned, "I'm hurt, Doc! Took a bullet. You gotta help me!"

There was a muffled oath from inside the hall and then Falcon heard the lock turn. The door opened and before the doctor could even recoil, Falcon jumped inside and pistol-whipped him just behind his left ear. Weaver collapsed in a heap, grabbing his head.

"Get up," Falcon ordered, "or I'll make you think I just gave you a friendly pat."

The doctor tried to stand, but when he had trouble, Falcon grabbed him by his shirtfront and hauled him to his feet.

"What do you want?" the doctor cried.

"I want Shiloh's head and you're going to help me get it."

"I don't know—"

Falcon jammed the barrel of his Colt in the doctor's belly. The doctor grunted and staggered.

"Horace!" a quavery voice cried from down the hall. "Is something wrong?"

Falcon grabbed the doctor and shoved him down the hall. "Let's go tell your little woman that everything is going to be just fine as long as you cooperate."

"Please, Edna is in poor health!" the doctor begged. "Leave her out of this!"

But Falcon shoved the man ahead until they came to the bedroom, then knocked the doctor to the floor. A skinny old woman opened her mouth to cry out in alarm, but Falcon silenced her by cocking back the hammer of his Colt.

"One scream," he warned, "and it'll be your last. And after I shoot you, Edna, I'll shoot your husband."

"What do you want?"

"I already explained that to the good doctor," Falcon said. "I want the man that is hiding in your little house out back. I want him here and now. He's too deadly to go in after."

"You want him brought to our bedroom?" The doctor's jaw dropped. "He won't—"

"He will," Falcon interrupted, cutting off the protest. "I don't care what you tell the man, but get him to come in here."

"But . . ."

"I'll give you fifteen minutes. If he isn't in here by then, I'll slit Edna's throat."

The old woman's hand fluttered to her mouth and her eyes widened with terror.

"You both heard me right," Falcon said to the doctor. "And if you warn him, I'll kill your wife, you and Shiloh, but not necessarily in that order."

"But what if he gets suspicious and won't come?"

"Then you're going to have a very messy bed," Falcon said without batting an eye.

Doc Weaver nodded. When he reached for his trousers, his hands were shaking as if he had the palsy.

"Get ahold of yourself, Doc! He sees you shaking like that, he'll know something is wrong and we've lost the game."

The doctor held up his shaking hands and then clasped them together very tightly in front of his eyes. When he parted them, they weren't shaking so badly.

"I'll do the best I can," he said, "but Shiloh is a very suspicious man and he knows that you've been following me. He's going to—"

Falcon pulled a knife from a sheath on his belt. He held the blade up to the light so that it glinted. "Just do what I told you and for the sake of your wife, you better pray that whatever you come up with to get the man in here works."

The doctor nodded, finished dressing and then left the room.

"You can kill me if you want," the old woman wheezed. "I'm nearly dead anyway. But don't you touch my husband! This town needs him!"

"Shut up," Falcon snapped. "I don't give a damn about you, him, or this town. All I care about is putting Shiloh down for keeps."

Tears welled up in the old woman's eyes. "I heard about men like you. You're evil!"

Falcon pressed the knife to the old woman's neck and touched it just hard enough to bring up a thin line of blood. "And you, old lady, are dead the next time you open your flappin' big mouth."

When he was certain that Edna wasn't going to ruin the surprise party, Falcon sheathed his knife and studied the dim bedroom, trying to decide where he would lie in wait. Behind the door was probably the best place. From there, he could step behind Shiloh with his gun in his hand and put two quick bullets into his unsuspecting body.

"Edna," he said, moving over to the door and easing in behind it, "if you even so much as look my way, or give any sign that this is where I'm waiting, I'll kill your husband with my first bullet. That's a promise."

"I despise you!" she said, bony hands knotted on her bedcovers and spittle flying. Her sunken eyes were as black as obsidian; Falcon had to admire anyone who could muster up that kind of pure hatred.

"And . . . and I think you're going to kill us all whether we cooperate with you or not!" Edna said defiantly.

"You'll live," Falcon said. "And since my word is the only hope you got for the moment, I suggest you had damn sure better do as I order."

She glared at him until he cocked his six-gun, then her nerve broke and she buried her face in her coverlet and wept piteously.

"Get ahold of yourself, Edna!" Falcon hissed. "They'll be in here any second."

Edna shuddered her entire wasted length, then she dried her tears on her nightgown sleeve, raised her head and composed her ravaged face.

For just an instant, it occurred to Falcon that when Edna had been young, she must have been damn pretty and spunky. Too bad she was going to die in the next few minutes; but then, judging from her appearance, there wasn't much left for her in this world anyhow.

11

WHEN THE KNOCK sounded on Shiloh's door, he came off the bed with his gun in his fist. Walking up to stand just to one side of the door, Shiloh said, "That you, Doc?"

"Of course it is! Open up!"

Shiloh unlocked the door. The moment he saw the doctor's stricken expression, he knew that something was terribly wrong.

"We need to talk," Weaver said.

"Come inside."

"No. We need to talk in my house."

Shiloh cast an eye toward the house. He'd never been invited in before and it was highly unusual that he would be now. Mrs. Weaver was not well, and up until now Shiloh had just naturally assumed that the doctor did not want his wife to be disturbed.

"Doc, come on inside and tell me what has gone wrong."

"Nothing!" The doctor lowered his voice. "Nothing is wrong, Shiloh. I just thought you might like to meet my wife, Edna."

"At seven-thirty in the morning?"

The doctor's composure began to crack. "Listen, just stop asking questions and come with me to the house."

The doctor even went so far as to turn and start back across the yard, but when Shiloh didn't budge, he rushed back. "Please!"

"He's got your wife under his gun, hasn't he."

The doctor tried to laugh but it didn't come out right. "No! Who?"

"Ballock's gunfighter. The one that I've been hiding from this past week. Falcon."

When the doctor started to deny that, Shiloh just reached out and grabbed the man by the shirtfront and hauled him inside. He closed the door behind the man and pushed him into his only chair.

"Doc, do you really think that Falcon will spare any of us? He's got to kill me, and once he does that he'll also have to kill you to eliminate any witnesses."

The doctor covered his face with his hands for a moment, then he shuddered and sighed. "You're the only one that poses him any danger!"

"But once I'm dead, you and your wife will also pose a threat. You'd be able to identify Falcon in a court of law. That means that he can't allow you to get out of this alive either."

The doctor wanted to protest, but he knew Shiloh was right. "All right," he whispered, "so what do we do?"

"Describe the layout."

"You mean the bedroom?"

"If that's where he is waiting."

"It's just an ordinary bedroom. The bed is directly across from the door. There are bedstands on each side of it and dressers on the left-hand wall. Closets on the right. The walls are covered with pictures."

"Could I see him if he was crouched low beside the bed?"

"I think you could," the doctor said.

Shiloh frowned. "What if he was under the bed? Is there

enough clearance for him to stick his gun out and shoot me as I walk in the door?"

"No. The footboard is too low and my wife has everything imaginable packed under the bed. I don't think he'd do that."

"Well," Shiloh said, "Falcon won't be standing in plain sight when I come into the room. I can tell you that much. What about the closets?"

"He might be able to climb into them and hide," the doctor admitted. "But it would be pretty cramped."

"And the closets are on the right side. My right coming in?"

"Yes."

"Where are the windows?"

The doctor was getting very anxious. "Falcon is going to get suspicious if we delay coming any longer! Can't we just—"

"Where are the windows?" Shiloh repeated in a firm voice.

"There is one over my beside stand. Another two or three along the same wall."

"All opposite the door?"

"Yes, yes! Now can't we—"

Shiloh had been pulling on his boots and strapping on his guns. "Let's go," he said, interrupting the doctor.

"But what are you going to do? You can't just go in there with guns blazing! He said that his first bullet would be for my wife!"

"He's lying," Shiloh said flatly. "He's got to kill me first. Then you, then your wife. He'll kill us in that order, leaving your wife until last. Do you have a gun?"

"No!" the doctor cried. "I've never even owned one."

"Here. Take one of mine," Shiloh said, handing the man one of his matched set of Colt revolvers. "Put it in your coat pocket. If I go down, at least you'll have a one-in-one-hundred chance."

"Against a man like that I'll have no chance!" The doctor

shoved the gun back at Shiloh. "You keep it!"

Shiloh retrieved his gun. He was disappointed in the doctor, and he had trouble understanding how any man could fail to want to have a fighting chance to save his own life.

"Let's go," Shiloh said, pulling on his hat and moving toward the door. "When we get to the house, I'm going to slip along the back to your bedroom window."

"You can't do that! You've got to come inside or my wife and I are dead!"

Shiloh ignored the man's plea. "When you go back into your bedroom, tell the gunman that I was sound asleep and am getting dressed. Tell him that I'll be along in a minute."

"But he won't—"

"Listen to me!" Shiloh ordered. "Falcon will be furious. He'll order you to come back here and bring me to the room."

"But—"

"And if he comes to the window to make sure that you do, I'll shoot him through the glass."

"You could miss!" The doctor began to shake his head. "And if you missed, my wife would be alone with that sonofabitch and he'd kill her in spite."

"I won't miss," Shiloh said. "Not if he gives me a clear target."

"But what if he doesn't!"

"I don't know," Shiloh admitted. "I can't promise you a damn thing. All I can say is that my idea is the best chance we have."

"It's your best chance! Not Edna's!"

"There's no time to argue about this," Shiloh said. "I'm a professional bounty hunter, you're a professional healer. This is my specialty, not yours. The only hope you or your wife has is to obey my orders."

"I should never have taken you in," the doctor said bitterly.

"I disagree, but there's no time for that now. Let's go."

The doctor wrung his hands. "If this fails . . ."

Shiloh prodded the man toward the door. If he gave himself a few minutes to think about it, he could get real worried and doubtful too. But in times like this, when a man had no choice but to act, it was best just to jump in with both feet and take care of business.

When they reached the back door, Shiloh gripped the doctor's arm. "Just do as I explained. He can't shoot you or your wife until he's got me for certain. He'll have no choice but to send you back outside for me."

The doctor nodded but he didn't look convinced. Shiloh pushed him through the door and then crouched a little, although that caused him an immense amount of pain. With his guns in his fist, he eased along the back of the house until he came to the doctor's bedroom window. Inside the house, Shiloh began to hear shouting and pleading. He removed his Stetson, raised up a little and peered through the corner of the window to see the dandy with a knife to the doctor's throat. Mrs. Weaver was in bed and was screaming at Falcon not to kill her husband.

Shiloh had a shot. It wasn't as good as he wanted, but it was a clear shot through the window. He took careful aim and then held his breath as he squeezed the trigger of his Colt.

The explosion, smoke and shattering glass obliterated everything from sight. Shiloh heard a high-pitched scream from the woman and then he started for the back door. He was just about to open it when two bullets ripped into the door.

Shiloh dropped to the back step, fired twice more and then waited. He could hear the old lady wailing for help. Shiloh couldn't bear to wait another second. Picking himself up, and expecting he'd probably die when he came through the doorway, he jumped. There were no shots. Just the woman's pitiful screams.

Shiloh sprinted down the hallway, sure that Falcon would

be holding Mrs. Weaver as a shield. But he was wrong. Falcon was gone, but not before he'd left the doctor choking in a pool of blood with his throat cut damn near from ear to ear.

12

SHILOH DROPPED TO the doctor's side, trying to drown out the sound of the woman's screams. The doctor was conscious, in fact was trying to get up, and he had the presence of mind to point toward his medical kit. Shiloh jumped for the black leather kit, his own mind a little dazed by the rapid and disastrous turn of events. He tore the medical kit open and held it up for the doctor, who reached inside and grabbed a pack of cotton bandaging. Almost instantly, the cotton was saturated with blood. The doctor began to point frantically toward the doorway. "Ma'am, what is he trying to tell me, dammit! Quit caterwauling and help or he's gone for certain!"

The woman threw herself out of bed. She looked down at her husband and Shiloh thought she was going to swoon. "Steady, ma'am! Does he want more bandaging?"

"Yes," she breathed. "That must be it! I know where he keeps everything."

"Then get it, quick!"

The doctor reached up with his left hand and stared at Shiloh, who could see that Weaver was struggling not only to breathe but also to keep from losing his mind in panic. Even as Shiloh watched, the doctor reached into his bag again and grabbed a forcep. He shoved it at Shiloh.

"What am I supposed to do with this?"

"Stop the bleeding!" Weaver gasped. "Pinch them . . . off!"

"But I'm no doctor!"

Weaver almost jammed the forcep up Shiloh's nose. "Just do it!"

Shiloh gulped and nodded his head. He took the forcep in his rough hand, feeling totally foolish and very clumsy. "I don't know what the hell I'm supposed to do with this damn tweezer," Shiloh confessed. "Doc, I can't see anything but blood and cut flesh."

At just that moment, the doctor's wife reappeared. She fell to her knees beside Shiloh and tore away the saturated cotton, then began to mop the wound clean with new bandaging.

"Right there, mister! Clamp that one!"

The old woman's finger was shaking badly but Shiloh could see which vessel she was pointing at and he clamped it off with the forcep.

"Now that one," the woman said, pointing to a second vessel that was squirting a thin stream of blood as she handed Shiloh another forcep.

Shiloh clamped it off too. "You act like you know what we're doing," he said to the old woman.

"I ought to," she snapped. "When I was young and steady, I helped my husband save lives on this damn western frontier for years."

Shiloh took hope. Under the woman's direction, he used every forcep in the doctor's kit and pretty near got all the bleeding stopped. He could see the doctor's ribbed windpipe. It had a thin slice, and each time the doctor exhaled it emitted little red bubbles with a whispering sound. Resting beside the windpipe, buried deep in muscle, was a major blue artery as big around as Shiloh's middle finger.

"If that was cut, he'd already be dead," Edna Weaver said, bending over and staring into her husband's pain-stricken eyes. "Darling, we're going to tie your bleeders off now with gut."

The doctor nodded. The woman turned her attention to Shiloh. She was very pale but her voice was steady and she was remarkably composed. "I hope you've got steady hands and nimble fingers."

"Couldn't we find someone else to do this?"

"No time. Besides, I can tell my husband has faith in you."

"I appreciate that, ma'am. I really do. But—"

"Now listen carefully," the woman said, overriding his objection. "I'll show you how to make a loop, then slip it over the forcep. Once that is done, you'll need to draw it down over to the tip and tie it off in a good knot that won't allow the bleeder to leak."

Shiloh sleeved sweat from his forehead. "It's easier to shoot a man than to fix him, that's for damn certain."

She paid him no attention but said to her husband, "It's going to be all right, darling. We're going to tie off the bleeders. But I don't know how to close up your windpipe." Doc Weaver crooked a finger and she bent close. Shiloh threw his head back and filled his lungs, steadying and mentally preparing himself for what he had to do next. He'd felt more relaxed going into a gun battle than he did right now.

The woman straightened. "My husband says that we should just put a gut stitch or two in his windpipe."

Shiloh stared at the white, bubbling windpipe. It made him feel a little squeamish and he was not a squeamish kind of man. "Are you sure that we can't just let it go? Maybe it would heal up just fine by itself."

"It would leak blood into his lungs and he'd drown within the hour."

"Oh." Shiloh expelled a deep breath. "If I've got to do it, then let's go. This ain't going to get any easier by waiting."

Edna reached into the doctor's kit and found a surgical needle and explained how to thread it. "Just pretend you're getting ready to mend a shirt."

"I don't mend them," Shiloh said. "I wear them till they rot on my back or get torn off, or I just wear them out and throw them away."

"Mr. Shiloh, just thread the damned needle," she ordered.

Shiloh threaded it, encouraged that his hands and fingers were steady.

"Now then," Edna told him, dabbing at the bloody wound and taking the threaded needle up with another forcep. "Use this and just hook that windpipe like you would the leather in a boot and pull the windpipe together."

"That's it?" Shiloh asked.

"I . . . I think so. Yes. I'm sure of it. But hurry! His breathing is already much worse!"

Shiloh agreed. He could hear a gurgling sound in the doctor's throat that had not been there a few minutes earlier. That told Shiloh that Doc Weaver's lungs were filling with blood. "Now I know why I'd rather shoot men than patch them up, ma'am," Shiloh said as he took a deep, steadying breath. He hooked the windpipe, and was surprised that it was as tough as the leather sole of his boots. "It don't want to go through."

"It *has* to go through! Push harder!"

He drove the surgical needle into the cartilage and it broke through. "Now what?"

"Twist it up with your wrist and bring it back through on the other side."

Shiloh did it.

"Good!"

"So what now?"

"Pull it up tight so that the opening is closed, then tie it in a knot."

Shiloh did as he was instructed. He could feel sweat popping out all over his body and the doctor was struggling to breathe.

VENGEANCE TRAIL

"Now," the woman said, "two more like it ought to be enough."

Shiloh used two more stitches to close the windpipe up as nice as could be and the awful whispering sound died.

"Now we can tie off the bleeders," the old woman said.

"All right. Show me what to do."

She showed him how to slip a loop over the forcep and onto the severed blood vessels where it could be tied in a single square knot. It was difficult at first, but became much easier toward the last.

"Maybe I missed my calling," Shiloh said when the last bleeder was knotted.

"I don't think so," Mrs. Weaver said. "And besides, we still have to sew up the neck itself."

"I forgot about that."

"That's why I don't think you missed your calling."

Shiloh found sewing up the sliced neck flesh to be much more tedious and exacting than tying off the blood vessels. He figured he must have spent two hours before the neck was closed up entirely. After that, the old woman doused the wound with iodine and told Shiloh how to bandage the neck. When it was over, Shiloh felt completely drained. He needed some fresh air in the worst way.

"You're going to be just fine," she said, kissing her husband's pale cheeks.

"You think he'll make it?" Shiloh asked, pushing to his feet.

"Thanks to you he will."

That simple statement and Mrs. Weaver's brave smile made Shiloh feel on top of the world. It made him feel as good as he'd felt about anything in a long, long time.

13

SHILOH WASHED HIS hands of the doctor's blood and dried them on a kitchen towel. "I'm mighty sorry things worked out this way for your husband. If he hadn't taken me in, then—"

"We needed the money," Mrs. Weaver interrupted. "We had some financial reverses. My husband is a fine doctor and a wonderful man, but he took me back East for treatment hoping I'd get better. It was very expensive and they couldn't do anything for me. It cost us everything except this house."

"I'm going to grab up my things," Shiloh said, "and I'll be finding another place to stay in Tuscorora."

"What about your wound?"

"It's about healed. A little sore and embarrassing, but other than that just fine."

"But where will you go?" She seemed genuinely concerned.

"To a hotel."

"But that awful man . . . he'll find you!"

"That's the idea, ma'am. Either that, or I'll find him.

Don't much matter. One of us is going to kill the other. I think I might have winged him through the window. I don't know. Either way, we're headed for a showdown."

"And so the killing and shooting goes on and on."

Shiloh heard the disappointment and resignation in Mrs. Weaver's voice. "Here," he said, taking a roll of money out of his pocket and peeling off some bills. "There's the hundred dollars I owe your husband for doctoring and giving me a place to hide and recover." He'd paid the doctor already, but Mrs. Weaver didn't have to know that.

"Thank you very much. I'm afraid a hundred dollars won't begin to cover the loss of income he'll suffer from this knife wound."

"You're right." Shiloh peeled off fifty dollars and stuck it into his pocket then and gave all the rest to the woman. "This ought to cover your expenses for quite some time, ma'am."

Mrs. Weaver kissed his cheek. "God bless you, young man. And though I'm a Christian, I pray that you kill that man instead of him killing you first. In fact, I hope you punch that devil a one-way ticket to hell!"

"I'll do my best," Shiloh promised. "So long."

Shiloh went out to the carriage house and gathered his things. He carried them around to Weed Street and found a new hotel. Shiloh's butt ached after walking for just a few blocks and he had a noticeable limp as he crossed the lobby to the registration desk.

"You got a man named Falcon staying in this hotel?" he asked the desk clerk as he flipped through the pages of the book.

"Falcon?"

"Probably ain't his real name," Shiloh explained. "He's a slender fella. A real dandy with a leather vest and a white Stetson that probably cost him twenty or thirty dollars. He might be wounded."

"Nope. I'd remember a man like that." The clerk looked

at Shiloh rather oddly. "I saw you limp across the lobby just now. Bad leg?"

"Something like that."

"Then I'll give you a room on the first floor so you won't have to climb the stairs."

"Much obliged," Shiloh said before paying the man and taking his room key.

That evening Shiloh went out and had himself a steak dinner, then he went to one of the saloons and, with his back to the wall, played some poker. Nothing very exciting, just two-bit ante stuff that did not completely occupy his mind so that he could keep part of his attention fixed on the door to the saloon in case Falcon suddenly appeared. But Falcon didn't appear that evening, and the next day Shiloh began to make the rounds of the hotels. There were four of them, but none had any boarders that matched Falcon's description.

"Well where else could the man be staying?" Shiloh asked with mounting exasperation. "I've visited every hotel in Tuscorora."

"Maybe he already left town."

"Yeah," Shiloh conceded. "That's a real possibility. But it don't strike me as being his style unless he was in bad shape. And since I know that the only doctor in town didn't treat him . . ."

"Oh," the clerk said, "Doc Weaver isn't exactly the only doctor in town."

"He isn't?"

"Well, he is and he isn't."

Shiloh was in no mood for riddles. "Speak it out short and plain," he demanded.

"Very well. What I'm trying to say is that there is a woman in town. Her name is Ramona. She's part Indian, part Mexican, part a lot of things, and she does a pretty good doctorin' business. Uses Indian medicines."

"The man I seek might have a bullet in his head. Can she handle that?"

The clerk nodded. "She's good with bullet wounds, snake

bites. Whatever. She might have treated the man that you're looking for."

"Where can I find her?"

"Ramona lives about a quarter mile east of town. You can't miss her house because it's the only one that is built round like a Navajo hogan. You ever seen one of them?"

"I have," Shiloh said. "And I thank you for your information."

After Shiloh had checked into his room and changed his bandage he limped back outside, and when he saw an ore wagon heading off toward the east of town, he hailed the driver. "Can I hitch a ride?"

"Fer two bits you can!"

"I got it," Shiloh said, climbing painfully up to sit beside the driver.

"Somebody catch you stealin' chickens and fill your ass with buckshot?" the driver asked with a barely concealed grin.

"Nope. It was a .45 caliber slug."

The driver's smirk died and he said with genuine concern, "That's hard, a man shootin' to kill another man over stealin' a damned chicken!"

Shiloh didn't bother to explain that his getting shot had nothing to do with chickens. He kept his eyes peeled for a hogan, and sure enough it stuck right out among the neighboring shacks and tents.

"This is far enough," he said to the driver. "Much obliged for the ride."

"I'll be comin' back in about two hours if you need another ride for two bits," the driver said hopefully.

"I'll keep it in mind," Shiloh said as he started for the hogan.

"Hello in there!" he called.

A moment later, a woman appeared. She was old and wrinkled but her eyes were about the prettiest shade of dark green Shiloh had ever seen in the face of a woman. "Are you Ramona?"

She nodded, then moved around us as if to circle him. Shiloh turned. "What . . ."

"You shot in ass?"

"Well, yeah, but that ain't the reason I'm here. You see—"

"Drop pants. I fix."

"Now wait a minute! I'm here looking for—"

"Drop pants!"

Shiloh didn't really feel like he had much choice but to drop his pants. The old woman grabbed the bandage and tore it off.

"Ouch! Take it easy back there!"

Ramona clucked her tongue. "Bad. Very bad. Need much medicine."

"The hell it does!"

"I make good for . . . ten dollars."

"It's just fine, I'm telling you!"

"Ass fall off soon."

Shiloh groaned. "Listen. It ain't gonna fall off. All I want to know is if you doctored a scrawny fella with a pitiful little blond mustache. He's got a skinny, wedge-like face and he wears a black vest and a pair of tan-colored boots. You fix this man?"

Ramona just stared at him.

"Well?"

"I fix you and then maybe we talk of this man."

"Just tell me this—did you see him? Is he wounded?"

Ramona's face was stone. "Come inside. Ten dollars save your ass."

Shiloh really saw no choice but to do as the woman ordered. "Damnation!" he swore before he pulled up his pants and tromped inside.

The interior of the hogan was filled with skinny, flea-and tick-infested dogs. There must have been twenty of them and the stench of dog piss and urp was so powerful that it almost gagged Shiloh. Some of the dogs rushed at him with wagging tails and licked his hands, others growled as if he were the long overdue meal they'd been expecting.

Shiloh batted the dogs away. There was a fire in the center of the hogan and its smoke was a welcome relief. Over the fire was a black kettle filled with steaming water.

"Pull down pants and lie flat, ass end up."

"Now wait a minute. I ain't lying down among all these pot-licking dogs! Anything you got to do, you do with me standing up in here or I'm leaving."

Ramona looked deep into his eyes. She must have sensed that Shiloh was not bluffing because she finally shrugged her shoulders as if she really did not care.

"What are you fixing to do?" Shiloh groused.

"You talk too much."

"Yeah! Well, I tell you what," Shiloh said, "why don't I pay you five dollars and you forget the medicine and just tell me what I want to know."

"Drop pants."

"Aw jeeezz!"

Shiloh dropped his pants again and the Indian woman kicked some of her starving dogs out of the way. Shiloh watched as she opened several leather bags and pulled out different sorts of leaves, grass and other mysterious things. "Why won't you at least tell me what you're going to do with all that?"

Ramona ignored him.

"Listen! I'll tell you something right now. If you think you're going to make me drink some damned concoction, forget it! I've had a hard enough time staying alive without letting you poison me!"

But the woman paid him no mind. Ramona packed all her little ingredients into a cloth sack about the size of a dinner plate and then she closed her eyes and began to chant. Her dogs set to howling and Shiloh stood with his pants down to his ankles and marveled at the messes he could get himself into without hardly trying.

At last, the woman and the dogs mercifully fell silent. Ramona held the bag of medicines up to the four winds and then she dropped it into the boiling water in the black kettle.

"Now wait a minute," Shiloh said, starting to see the shape of things to come.

But the woman paid him no mind. She stirred the cloth bag around, chanting and singing with a few of the dogs yipping and still raising hell. When she fished the cloth bag out with a pair of wooden sticks, she held it dripping and steaming up between them and, for the first time, she grinned.

"Good medicine save your ass!"

Shiloh realized the old woman was missing all her teeth. "Yeah," he said, "I'm sure it is. But . . . get that away from me!"

But the old medicine woman would not be denied. Dangling the steaming poultice between them, Ramona advanced until Shiloh turned and bolted for the door. Unfortunately, he tripped over one of the mongrels and went sprawling into the doorway.

Ramona pounced on him like a cougar. The steaming poultice seared his wounded buttock. "Ahhh!" Shiloh cried. "Damn you!"

The woman and her dogs surged all over him, some of the dogs licking his face, others nipping at his ears. Shiloh covered his head and gritted his teeth. He knew that this humiliation would last only as long as the heat in the poultice. He was right. When the poultice cooled, Shiloh felt the weight of Ramona and her dogs fall away. He jumped up, grabbed his pants and buckled them around his waist.

"Dammit, old lady, if you were a man, I'll kill you *and* those flea-bitten mongrels!"

"Ten dollars fix very good now."

"What about the man I described? What about the dandy? Did you fix him up too?"

In reply, the old woman held out her hand and Shiloh had no choice but to pay her. She counted the bills, and when she was satisfied, she said, "I fix him good for twenty dollars. Bullet go through mouth."

"What?"

She placed an index finger on each cheek and opened her mouth to indicate what had happened.

"You mean I shot him through the cheeks?"

Ramona nodded. "Tongue gone. Some teeth too. Very bad."

"Where did he go from here?"

She shrugged.

"When did he leave?"

"Morning."

"Did you see if he rode back to Tuscorora or—"

The woman pointed to the town. Shiloh had been hoping she'd point north, back toward Chili Gulch. If she had, he'd have said the hell with it all and let the man go. But if Falcon was man enough to remain in Tuscorora in the hope of putting a bullet in his gizzard, Shiloh figured he would stay and try his damnedest to return the favor.

14

FALCON WAS IN torment. He'd seen the hole in his face, and he'd spat blood for hours waiting to see if he would live or die. The medicine woman had saved his life by giving him a packet of bitter herbs to suck on and the herbs had finally stopped the bleeding. Now Falcon waited for Shiloh to appear in the street below. All that was required was just one or two seconds for Falcon to get the man in the sights of his rifle, and that would be enough. Just a lonely second or two.

Once, earlier that afternoon, Falcon had actually seen Shiloh limping across Weed Street. But by the time he could line the man up in his sights, Shiloh had stepped under the overhang of the porch just below and vanished.

Tears of bitterness and rage filled his eyes because his face was ruined. He was going to be a freak whose disfigurement would cause women to shrink back in fear. And his tongue was now a large, mutilated mass of flesh. Falcon doubted that he would ever again be able to speak. It would have been better, far better, if he'd died in that first attack Shiloh had unleashed through the doctor's bedroom window. At least he had paid the doctor for his treachery. Probably it had been the sight of the doctor that had unnerved Shiloh, or at least distracted him from taking up an immediate chase. Falcon didn't care. His life was over. All he wanted to do was to kill Shiloh and then maybe kill himself rather than become an object of ridicule.

As time passed and the afternoon grew long, Falcon took a measure of hope. Maybe, if he lived to kill Shiloh, he could regain his speech. And as for his poor cheeks, a good surgeon might be able to sew them up so that the scars would not be too visible. But everything now depended on killing Shiloh.

Just before sundown, Falcon, who had been dozing a little because he was weakened by loss of blood, saw Shiloh reappear in the street and begin to cross it, moving toward the Big Bear Saloon. Falcon raised his Winchester, squinting into the sun, which was low and bothered his eyes. He sighted the rifle and, just as Shiloh was about to enter the saloon, squeezed the trigger.

The slug hit Shiloh in the cartridge belt and spun him completely around. As he spilled into the doorway Falcon levered the rifle and fired swiftly, but he knew he'd missed because Shiloh was gone. He choked with fury, spitting out his bloody herb pack. Falcon jumped to his feet, levering another shell into his rifle. He took aim on the front window of the Big Bear Saloon and shot it out.

He wanted to yell a challenge for Shiloh to come and get him if he still had the guts for it. But since he could only make a strangled, unintelligible sound, Falcon just stood there in full view, daring his hated enemy to come and make it a good fight.

Shiloh's left leg was numb from the hip down. Falcon's bullet had ripped through his cartridge belt, and when the man had blown out the saloon's window it had covered Shiloh with glass.

VENGEANCE TRAIL 101

"Sonofabitch!" someone in the saloon shouted. "What is going on?"

Shiloh eased back from the window. With the numbness in one leg and the ache in his butt, he was barely able to cross the saloon to the bar.

"Give me a whiskey!" he ordered.

The bartender slammed a bottle down in front of him. "That window is worth fifty dollars!"

"I'll get it off the bastard who shot it out," Shiloh promised as he upended the bottle and gulped the liquor down until he felt the pain ease. "You got a back door?"

"Sure, but . . ."

Shiloh hobbled toward it. "Hey! What about the whiskey and the window!"

At the back door, Shiloh stopped and turned. "Mister," he said, "I'm going to kill the snake that has put me in so much physical misery that I can barely get around. As you can plainly see, I'm not in the best of shape, so I could use a scattergun if you've got one to loan."

"I got one, but I'll be damned if I'll give it to you!" Shiloh drew his six-guns and pointed them at the bartender. "I mean to borrow that scattergun with or without your permission. What's it to be?"

"All right!" the bartender cried. "Take it easy!"

"Just bring it up nice and slow," Shiloh ordered. "Butt first." The bartender did as he was told and Shiloh limped over and retrieved the shotgun. It was double-barreled and loaded with heavy buckshot. Shiloh nodded with approval. "I'll bring it back shortly," he promised.

"You'd damn sure better!"

Shiloh swung the shotgun around in the man's general direction, and the bartender must have thought he was about to be shot because he dropped from sight behind the bar faster than if someone had chopped off his legs. Shiloh limped out into the alley. He was hoping that Falcon was still on the same rooftop but he doubted it.

When Shiloh rounded the corner and came back onto

the main street, he glanced up to the roof and wasn't a bit surprised to see that Falcon was gone. Shiloh looked to the west and saw that there was less than a half hour of daylight remaining. He wanted to get Falcon in the worst way before it got dark, but to do so would mean taking a few chances.

"To hell with it," Shiloh muttered, hobbling across the street, the scattergun pointed up toward the rooftop.

He reached the other side of the street and entered the nearest building, which was a rambling old general store. "I need to get up on your roof," he said to a man with a flowing handlebar mustache who wore a clerk's apron. "Have you got an inside stairwell?"

"No, sir! It's outside in the back."

"Show me the way," Shiloh ordered.

"Now listen, mister. I don't want to get involved in any shoot-out! I got a wife and two kids!"

"Just show the damned staircase to me!" Shiloh snapped, turning the barrel of the scattergun in the clerk's direction.

"Yes, sir!"

A minute later Shiloh was standing alone beside the stairs looking up at the rooftop. This was not the same building from which Falcon had staged his ambush, but it was right next door. Shiloh was in agony as he climbed the stairs, and even though it was cool outside he was sweating profusely when he edged his head up over the flat rooftop. To Shiloh's utter amazement, Falcon was sitting cross-legged with his rifle. When he saw Shiloh, he brazenly motioned for him to come forward.

Shiloh climbed up on the roof. Except for a big stovepipe, there was absolutely nothing that would serve as cover, and he did not much like the idea of matching a scattergun against a Winchester over anything more than a very short distance.

"I'm damn glad that I shot you in the face!" Shiloh called, coming to his feet and limping across the roof so he could be as near to Falcon as possible. "I don't expect you to be able to answer, but before the party begins I want you to know that I practiced a little throat surgery after you ran out on me over at the doc's house. The doc is going to be just fine. And I'll tell you one other thing—you ain't going to be fine at all in about fifteen seconds."

Falcon's ruined face twisted with hatred and he threw the Winchester to his shoulder. Shiloh didn't bother even to do that much, instead firing both barrels from waist high. As he dropped the empty scattergun and reached for his Colts, he saw Falcon's body explode like the pulp of a watermelon as the heavy shot ripped him apart. Shiloh's guns were up and pointed but he didn't need to empty them. Falcon's face had not been pretty moments earlier, and now it was downright disgusting.

Shiloh holstered his six-guns and picked up the scattergun. Grunting with pain, he turned away from the bloody mess lying on the next rooftop and hobbled back down the stairs. When he reentered the Big Bear Saloon, he dropped the empty scattergun on the bar.

"What about damages for my windows?" the bartender snarled.

"You can get them off the man up on that rooftop if you've got the stomach for it," Shiloh said. "And if he ain't got nothing in his pockets, you ought to be able to sell his rifle and Colt for a pretty fair piece of change."

"Now wait a minute! I don't . . ."

Shiloh wasn't listening. His bottle of whiskey was still standing on the bar and he snatched it up and then limped back out the front door as men cleared him a wide path.

It was finished. Shiloh hoped that now he could get himself healed up and go on to Virginia City since his luck had not been worth a damn in this part of the country. Shiloh raised the bottle and drank to ease his pain. Up and down the street men and women stared at him as if he were some kind of oddity never before seen in Tuscorora.

That rankled Shiloh. "Go on about your damned business!" he shouted. "If you want to see something that'll churn the belly of a buzzard, climb up on that roof yonder!"

They looked up, following his raised finger, and Shiloh upended the bottle again thinking it was high time he got drunk. But a voice from just behind him coupled with the familiar sound of a Colt cocking brought that pleasant line of thinking to a sudden halt.

"Shiloh," the voice said as a gun poked him hard in the ribs, "I been waitin' for this moment a long, long time. So let's you and me go nice and easy and take a little walk back into the alley."

Shiloh started to turn but changed his mind when the man hissed, "Just keep your hands from your guns and walk, you sonofabitch!"

Shiloh began hobbling painfully down the boardwalk and then into the corridor between the buildings as he headed toward the alley. "Who the hell are you?"

"You'll see," the voice said, "but not out here."

Shiloh's mind was racing now. It was very dim between the buildings, and the man kept so close that pressure from the muzzle of his gun never eased up on Shiloh's back. When they entered the alley, the man said, "Reach for the sky and turn around slow."

Shiloh reached and turned. "You're the one that got away during the blizzard," he said, recognizing the youngest of the brothers.

"That's right. You shot Matt and Clete to death in that line shack."

"They needed shooting," Shiloh said matter-of-factly. "I sort of thought a little better of you, being the youngest and all. I figure we should just let bygones be bygones."

Jess shook his head. "No sir! I been waiting for this moment ever since and I just wish that I could kill you slow."

"Well, maybe you can," Shiloh said, trying to buy time. "It's when a man hurries that he gets in trouble. If you have such a hatred for me that it churns your guts, I'd say the best thing to do would be to take me off somewhere and peel my hide. You can't do that here, though. Not with the whole town stirred up the way it is right now."

Jess stepped back, a twisted smile on his face. He raised his pistol. "Say your prayers, you bastard."

Shiloh reckoned maybe saying his prayers was about the only thing he could do except for making a play for his guns and hoping for a miracle. He was just about to do both when a crowd of excited townspeople rounded the corner of the alley looking for the stairs that would take them up to see Falcon's body.

"Hey," the lead man shouted, peering into the failing light, "what the . . . !"

Shiloh threw himself behind a rain barrel as Jess opened fire. The barrel sprouted leaks. Men shouted and dove for cover as Shiloh rolled on his bad hip, grunted with pain and then dragged his gun up and began slamming shots into Jess, who seemed paralyzed with shock and confusion.

The young man danced in the twilight as each of Shiloh's bullets impacted his body, turning it one way and then the next. Jess fired twice more, once at the ground and then finally at the red orb of the dying sun before he pitched forward, dead before he struck the alley.

Shiloh climbed to his feet and stood in the swirling gunsmoke. No one said a word as he reloaded from his cartridge belt and then hobbled off to get a fresh bottle of whiskey.

15

IT TOOK A week before Shiloh could walk straight upright. It took another week before he judged that he could sit in a saddle long enough to reach Virginia City. During that time, he visited Doc Weaver and his wife most every day and while the doc's voice was quite weak, it had returned almost immediately.

"It's either a medical miracle," the doc said the day that Shiloh was planning to ride out, "or else you and the missus have the makin's of the best surgical team west of the Mississippi."

Mrs. Weaver smiled. She looked much better now that her husband's life was clearly out of danger. "Shiloh has good steady hands. I doubt any woman ever made a nicer stitch than he made in your windpipe."

"He did a fine job," the doc said. "Shiloh, you're still a young fella. I could write a few letters and see about getting you into an eastern medical school. Maybe even Harvard, where I graduated a good many years ago."

"No, sir," Shiloh said, "I just don't think I'm cut out to be a doctor or a surgeon."

"How can you say that? From what Edna has told me, you performed brilliantly. You've obviously the dexterity as well as the instincts of a good all-around surgeon."

"I just wouldn't like it," Shiloh confessed, "though I have the greatest admiration for men such as yourself."

"Is it that you can't read or write?"

"No, sir!" Shiloh said, slightly offended. "I can read and write just fine. It's just that I couldn't abide living in the East or doing that studying. I went to school long enough to know I'm no scholar."

The doc nodded with reluctant impatience. "Well, I can appreciate that we are all different. But being a bounty hunter seems a hard and dangerous livelihood and I'd like to see you do better."

"I do just fine, Doc. I live outdoors. I travel wherever I want, and the men that I hunt are usually raising so much hell that when I capture or kill them, everyone is pretty damned grateful. I like my line of work and there are none better."

Mrs. Weaver said, "Someday you'll go after a man and he'll wind up killing you!"

"That might happen," Shiloh admitted, "but life out west is always a gamble."

The doctor winked. "I can see right now that the missus and I are not going to get you to change your mind and think about medical school or even settling down in Tuscorora."

"No, sir," Shiloh said. "As much as I enjoy your company and the pleasures of this town, I am getting pretty restless. It's time to move on."

"What about those folks up at the Lazy B ranch?" the doc asked. Shiloh had confided the reasons for his being pursued to Tuscorora.

"Well, sir, since there isn't a bounty on Horatio Ballock's head that I know of, and since I've already killed a fair passel of his men including his son, I just think I'll let the while thing pass."

"Wise decision," the doc said agreeably. "I've heard plenty about Horatio Ballock. Thankfully, I've never had to deal with him or his men. They have a very bad reputation."

"Someone will pull that old bull down one of these days," Shiloh said. "Usually it's one of his own men that will end up running things."

"Do you really believe that a man like Horatio Ballock will just let you ride off scot-free?"

Shiloh shrugged. "Well, sir, he sent his son, that Jess fella, and even his best shooter after me. I was good enough to kill all of 'em and I got to believe that, sooner or later, even a man like Ballock has to call it quits."

"A man that ruthless and powerful isn't the type to call anything quits," the doc argued. "I think it's fortunate that you are leaving today."

"So do I," Edna said. "It's bound to be healthier for you, Shiloh."

Shiloh nodded and unfolded out of an easy chair. He had been sipping tea in their parlor but the tea was gone and there was nothing left to say. "Thanks again for everything."

"Thank you," they told him.

Shiloh left the house and walked out to his horse. He was still limping noticeably, but the doctor had examined his hip and his buttock and pronounced him fit for travel. There would be some pain and stiffness for a few weeks and then he'd be fine.

"You stop by if you ever pass through, hear me!" the doc hollered. "But not if you're in trouble again!"

Shiloh chuckled and waved good-bye, then grunted as he eased into his saddle and rode west, heading for the Comstock Lode.

The weather had cleared and the snow had melted. A warm, blustery wind caressed Shiloh's face and he felt pretty damned good considering all the punishment he'd taken in Chili Gulch and Tuscorora. He was nearly broke again, but there was always money to be made for an enterprising man and no better place to make it than the Comstock.

That night and the one that followed, Shiloh skirted little mining towns whose lights shone brightly in the distance. He was fed up with people and was enjoying his own company. He was little money but he'd had the foresight to buy enough grain and supplies to keep himself and the liver chestnut happy. His pace was deliberate, but unhurried. Perhaps a half dozen times a day he chanced upon a couple of hard-rock miners working their staked claims, and he tried to avoid them as much as possible.

Shiloh was always careful to make his presence known among prospectors because, as a general rule, they were about the most suspicious folks on earth. When you chanced upon a lonely prospector, no matter how poor his claim, he just naturally assumed you would kill him for the gold that surely was about to be found. Prospectors were a strange, solitary breed. Hard men, usually tetched in the head by gold fever and the blazing desert sun. Shiloh had never understood prospectors and thought them all crazy. Why else would they endure the hardship and loneliness unless they were a little batty.

He was thinking this one sunny afternoon when, in the distance, he saw the wispy plume of a campfire. Shiloh could see a burro standing near the fire but he could not see its owner. Good sense and past experience told him to make a wide loop around the camp, but a buzzard circling overhead told him that something might be wrong so he reined his horse to a standstill.

"Hello up there the camp!" His voice echoed over the barren hills and Shiloh called again. No answer.

"I'm coming in!" Shiloh eased a six-gun up a little from the resting place in his holster. He kept his eyes on the burro, sure that if there was someone sneaking around the campfire waiting to ambush the first passerby, the burro would betray his movement.

But the burro just stood with its head down looking thin and forlorn. As Shiloh drew closer, he could see that the animal was hobbled. Shiloh rode into the camp, noting mine tailings and a hole in a sage-covered hillside. His eyes missed nothing but he still could see no sign of a prospector.

"He's probably in the mine," Shiloh said to himself, dismounting to tie his reins to a piece of brush.

He walked up to the mine and was immediately overpowered by the stench of death. Shiloh turned away and lit a match, then took a deep breath and entered the mouth of the little tunnel. He had to bend over in a crouch to move forward and the stench grew stronger with every step he took.

Shiloh thought he was going to gag to death before he came to the end of the tunnel and saw a half-decomposed body that greeted him with empty eyes. Shiloh knelt beside the body and saw the bullet hole in the man's chest. The face was in an advance state of decay, but it appeared to Shiloh that the man had been in his fifties, perhaps even older because his hair was white. Looking around, Shiloh found a spent shell from a Winchester and he saw that the face of the wall had a promising vein of quartz. He knew that gold was often found among quartz formations, but another match did not reveal any trace of ore. There was an old kerosene lantern and Shiloh used it to have an even better look around.

"I don't know what they killed you for," he said, feeling almost faint because of the stench, "but I'm going to bury you where you lay."

Shiloh staggered outside to where he'd seen a pick and shovel. Forcing himself to go back into the tunnel wasn't easy but he did it, and within a very few minutes he had covered up the body with loose quartz rock. It wasn't much of a burial, but Shiloh was afraid that the partially decomposed body would pull apart if he tried to drag it outside.

Thoroughly bushed by his efforts and feeling a little sick to his stomach, Shiloh decided to use this camp to boil himself some coffee and fry some potatoes. Whoever had killed the man in the mine hadn't bothered to take anything, and there were several frying pans and pots to use.

Shiloh stoked up the campfire and put a pot of water on to boil. He went over and removed the hobbles from the poor, half-starved burro. It was a friendly little critter and showed its gratitude by nuzzling Shiloh's hand.

"You're free," Shiloh said. "Go join a mustang band or find some of your own kind. There's plenty that have been cut loose or run away."

But the burro stayed that night. He kept a vigil beside the campfire and around midnight brayed mournfully at the moon. It was then that Shiloh understood that the poor beast was lonesome for its dead master.

At first light, Shiloh arose feeling somewhat restless. He'd had his dreams again and had not slept well. Now, he was anxious to be on his way and put this death camp far behind him.

"Vamoose!" he shouted at the burro, trying to drive it away before he left. But the burro just rolled its large brown eyes at him and stood spraddle-legged, head down.

"Damn," Shiloh said, uncoiling the lariat tied to his saddle, "you look so sorry that I expect you'll stand there and just die if I was to leave you behind."

Shiloh was not a great hand with a rope, but it was hard to miss a stationary target so he did get the loop over the burro's furry head. Dallying his loop around his saddlehorn, Shiloh led off to the west. The burro dug in its heels and had to be dragged for about forty feet before it realized that it was helplessly overmatched against a full-sized horse.

Braying with distress and sorrow, the burro fell in behind the horse and Shiloh lined out toward the Comstock. He had seen enough death on the frontier not to be overly concerned with the murder he'd uncovered in that gold mine. Maybe there had been gold there and he'd missed it—entirely

16

OUT OF FOOD and weary of the company of his horse and the braying burro, Shiloh rode into Hoochville late one afternoon. It wasn't much of a town, just a single hotel, livery, three saloons and a couple of dry-goods stores and places to eat. That was fine with Shiloh. His first stop was at the livery.

"Your gelding needs a new set of shoes," the liveryman said. "I can tack on a set for five dollars."

"They're going to have to wait," Shiloh said, counting the few dollars remaining in his pants. "Just feed the chestnut well."

"What about that little burro? He looks to be half starved."

"I'd like to sell him," Shiloh said. "He ought to be worth twenty dollars to a prospector."

"If you can get ten, take it."

Shiloh did not want to hear this. "What will you pay for him?"

"Five would be about all I could offer."

"Eight and that's the very least I'll take," Shiloh said.

"Seven dollars is my top offer."

Shiloh did not even have enough money for a night's lodging and a couple of good meals. "Seven dollars and fifty cents and you've got yourself a hell of a good burro. Probably make ten dollars profit on him at least."

The liveryman nodded and paid Shiloh, who said, "Where's the best place to eat in this town?"

"There ain't none."

"Well, where is the best of the worst then?"

"George's Café would be the one least likely to poison a man. You can't miss it."

"Thanks," Shiloh said, "and feed them two animals well. They've had a long, hard trail."

"Burro especially," the liveryman said. "He looks like he's half starved to death."

Shiloh did not tell the man the sad story about the burro's real owner. He figured that it might just raise a question about his own right to sell the little critter. And since he needed the money, he wasn't about to take any chances.

Shiloh paid for a hotel room that included six other men sleeping on cots, and then he bought a few badly needed supplies before his appetite got the best of him.

George's Café was a sorry establishment even by frontier standards. The kitchen was outdoors and consisted of a wood fire in a bathtub with a couple of iron griddles laid across the top. You could watch George frying your beefsteak and potatoes, sweat dripping on the food, a continuous stream of curses on his lips as he chewed the stump of a cheap Mexican cigarillo.

The steak that Shiloh ordered was barely edible and the potatoes were burned, but the coffee was surprisingly good and contained not more than a tablespoon of grounds.

"How about some pie?" Shiloh asked.

"Dollar a slice."

"To hell with it."

When Shiloh paid his bill, he had only two dollars left to his name. It was barely enough to get him into anything but possible because his eye was not trained to detect ore. Still, he'd not have remained there a single extra day to work a dead man's mine. Call it superstitious, but neither would Shiloh have dug up a cemetery for gold.

the smallest stakes poker game, and if he didn't win right away he'd be finished. Maybe even reduced to swamping out spittoons for a few lousy dollars a week.

Shiloh found the kind of hard-luck game that he was searching for, but sometimes a man's luck stayed cold. At the end of two hands, Shiloh was busted.

"Got a pretty good knife," he said, pulling it from his boot and laying it flat on the table. "You won't find a better quality of steel."

"Give you three dollars," a fat man across from him grunted.

"I gave twenty dollars for that knife!" Shiloh protested.

"Ain't worth no twenty dollars to me, friend."

Shiloh looked to the rest of the card players, who were as disreputable a bunch as you could find anywhere on the frontier. "What about you other fellas? You won't find a better knife anywhere for less than twenty dollars."

"Are we playin' cards, or what?" one of the men asked beligerently. "Either take the man's three dollars, or put the damn knife back in your boot and let somebody with money fill your seat."

"All right! I'll take the three dollars, but it is damned low to take a knife this good for three crummy dollars."

Nobody cared. Shiloh took the three dollars and lost it in the next half hour. Angry with himself for being foolish to gamble when his luck was running bad, he stomped out of the saloon and went to the hotel, where he stretched out on a cot with his bedroll and promptly went to sleep, even though it was only a little past sundown.

He awoke sometime in the night hearing the man next to him vomiting on the floor. He went back to sleep but was knocked off his cot just before dawn by a pair of drunken miners who got into a wrestling match that soon turned nasty when one gouged the other in the eyeball. There was a lot of cussing and howling before the pair was ejected into the street.

"Sonsabitches got no respect for another man's sleep!"

Shiloh growled, climbing back on his cot.

He lay down and closed his eyes, thinking he should have slept out in the sagebrush again. He must have drifted off to sleep because when he opened his eyes, the sun was high and he was the only man left in the room. Unfortunately, all his supplies were gone, as were his hat and boots.

"Sonofabitch!" he swore in anger, pulling his guns out of his bedroll and looking for someone to shoot.

Of course, there wasn't anyone to shoot and he only had himself to blame for his sorry predicament. That was the way of it when a man was down so low he had to sleep with six thieves in a room. Furious at the way things had gone in this town, Shiloh walked on tender feet back to the stable where he explained his sad situation.

"You want to sell that horse and saddle, we might be able to make a deal."

"How much for the pair?"

"Twenty dollars, tops."

"Tops!" Shiloh exclaimed. "Why, mister, I admit I'm in a fix, but I'd starve before I'd sell a horse and saddle of that quality for less than forty dollars."

"Thirty and that's as much as I can go, and I'm probably getting skinned."

"Thirty-five and you've got the finest saddlehorse in this piss-poor town."

They settled on thirty-two fifty and Shiloh walked down to the nearest general store and used all but three dollars of his money to buy another Stetson and a pair of boots that were too damned tight and pinched his toes, but were the only ones that were available.

He headed on foot toward the road leading out of town where, with a little luck, he could hitch a ride to the Comstock. Maybe he'd have to feed the team or do some work to help pay for his ride, but anything was better than rotting in Hoochville another miserable day.

Shiloh was standing out by the road when a group of five riders appeared.

"Afternoon!" one of them called real friendly like.

"Afternoon."

"Stuck for a ride, huh?" the leader said.

"Yeah. I've had a little bad luck lately. It'll change though."

The man and his friends suddenly drew their pistols. "Not today it won't."

Shiloh's hands were on the butts of his six-guns, but he knew he'd be signing his death warrant if he drew on the riders.

"Raise your hands, Shiloh!"

"Who the hell are you?"

"My name is Art Lee. I'm foreman of the Lazy B ranch." The man smiled. "I'm sure you can figure out why we came looking for you."

Shiloh felt a chill pass up his spine, but he had no intention of showing his fear. With a grin on his face, he said, "I think I can guess, Mr. Lee. Old Horatio Ballock decided that he wanted to send you out to repay me for all the trouble he put me through in Chili Gulch."

"That's right," the man said. "Now we can do this real hard or real easy. How do you want it to go?"

Shiloh looked at their grim faces. "What's real hard mean?"

"It means I shoot you in both kneecaps and then we lash you over a saddle and haul your bleeding ass to the ranch."

"Doesn't sound too good," Shiloh said. "And real easy is if I do exactly what you say. Right?"

"Right. So you can just ease those fancy pistols out of your holsters and drop them to the dirt."

Shiloh did as he was told. They had him dead to rights and he'd be a fool to make a play while his luck was running bad.

"Now what?"

"Put your hands up high."

Shiloh raised his hands. Art Lee climbed down from his

horse and stepped up to Shiloh. "Turn around and cross your wrists behind your back."

"Yes, sir," Shiloh said in his most agreeable tone of voice.

Lee bound his wrists together and then ordered one of his cowboys to dismount so that Shiloh could take his place. When Shiloh was mounted, his new boots were tied together under the horse, so that if he tried to jump off he'd be whipped underneath the animal. The horse would bolt in fear and run and he'd be beaten to death by its iron-capped hooves. It was exactly how Shiloh would have handled things had he been the one taking a hostage.

"We heading back to the ranch right away?" he asked conversationally.

"That's right."

"Good," Shiloh said in a hearty voice. "I'm anxious to meet the ornery old sonofabitch. Everyone tells me he's got more venom in him than ten fair-sized rattlers."

Lee didn't grin, but he had to struggle to keep a straight face. "The old man has some pretty rough ways, and you killing his son did not improve his disposition."

"His son gave me no choice. He came looking for me, not the other way around. I only did what any man would do to keep breathing. I shot him in self-defense."

"Tell that to Mr. Ballock," Lee said, kicking his foot out of his stirrup so that the cowboy whose horse Shiloh now sat could ride double.

They headed off then, skirting Hoochville and moving briskly to the northeast. There was a long ride ahead of them that would take two, maybe even three days, no matter how fast they traveled. Shiloh was feeling low-spirited and hoping his bad luck was going to change. It had to change soon or he was a goner.

"Mr. Ballock says you must be one hell of a fighter," the rider on Shiloh's left said. "I sure wish I could have braced you by myself. Would have made my reputation."

Shiloh looked at the young man's arrogant, smirking

face. "It would have made you a corpse."

The gunman's smirk evaporated. "You ain't so tough. We took you easier than if we'd braced some poor drunk on the street. I was expecting something special but you didn't even have a damned horse."

Shiloh turned away from the man. Let him think what he wanted. Somehow, in the next couple of days, he would do his damnedest to teach the hired gunman the deadly meaning of reality.

17

LATE THAT AFTERNOON, they stopped at a little trading post and general store on the banks of a fair-sized stream. There was a corral full of horses, but most of them looked old or lame.

"Let's see if they've got one for Joe. Riding double is about to do my horse in," Art Lee said.

"They're a sorry bunch," one of the Lazy B riders commented. "Ain't a one of them I'd be willing to show Horatio."

"He won't care what we buy or pay as long as we hand over Shiloh to him," Lee said. "That's all he thinks about right now."

They tied their horses up to the hitch rail and Shiloh was pushed headlong into the store. There wasn't much of anything for sale, and it was clear that the fat man who greeted them was hoping they'd drink his home-brewed whiskey.

"Best old firewater in Nevada," the man boasted, ignoring the fact that Shiloh was bound by his wrists. "Fifty cents a shot and I'll guarantee you that you won't ride away sober if you have more'n three drinks."

"We'll have none," Lee said.

There were some groans and even outright bitching at this piece of news, but the Lazy B riders did not challenge the edict. They seemed to know that crossing their foreman was the same as crossing Horatio Ballock.

All this Shiloh observed quietly as he watched and waited, hoping for a chance to escape with his life. Several of the men were quite young, barely out of their teens. They were brash and swaggering youths, and Shiloh knew they were the most likely to make a serious mistake that could be used to his advantage.

The store owner could not hide his disappointment. "Well, then, if you boys ain't drinkin', I got some cigars and a few canned goods on the shelves."

"Damned few," one of the men complained.

"What we need," Lee said, "is an extra horse. It doesn't have to be a trained cow pony or even a quality animal, but it does have to be sound."

"Oh, I got lots of sound horses," the man said, hopeful again. "And I saw you and that other fella ridin' double up here and then I said to myself, 'Ernie, them boys need a good horse.' That's what I said."

"Why don't we go outside and see if there's anything out there that would fit the bill," Lee said, heading for the door and prodding Shiloh along before him.

"What's that one tied up for? He a horse thief, or what?"

"That and a murderer," Lee said as they passed outside, moving toward the corral.

They all crowded around the pen, studying the sorry collection of horses. Art Lee shook his head. "The only animal worth throwin' a saddle over is that bay gelding with the blazed face and two white stockings."

Ernie wagged his chins. "Why, you sure do have a good eye for horseflesh, sir! Yes you do! That is by far the best horse in the bunch. They say he's a little rough to ride, but he can outrun anything with four legs in the territory. None faster."

"He looks fast, but if you have him he must have some problems," Art Lee said.

"Oh," the man said, "he's hardly more than a colt and full of piss and brimstone. But he just needs a little work to round off the rough edges. That's all."

"Sure," Lee growled.

"It's true! And of course, I did have to pay double what I paid for them others."

Lee did not even look at the man. "He's worth thirty and that's what I'll pay for him."

"Oh no, sir!" the store owner cried. "That horse cost me fifty dollars! And I been feeding him for a month! Why, I'd be losing money if I sold him to you for less than . . . sixty."

Lee glanced at the cowboy whose horse Shiloh had taken. "Joe, get a rope on him and then find an extra bridle and ride him bareback."

"Why can't Shiloh ride bareback!" Joe protested. "Either that, or give me back my own damn saddle."

"All right," Lee said after a long pause. "Shiloh, you ride this bay horse bareback."

"Suits me," Shiloh said, "but I can't do it with my hands and ankles tied."

"Yes you can," Lee said.

"But if the horse bolts and I slip off his back . . ." Shiloh didn't have to finish because it was obvious what would happen to him.

"That's right," Lee said. "If you fall you'll probably get your head beat in."

"Mister," the storekeeper was saying, "I just can't sell that animal for no thirty dollars! I *won't* sell him for that kind of money."

Lee turned on the fat man. "Don't tell me you won't do something, mister. You've just sold him so get your fat ass into that two-bit store of yours and write out a receipt. I'll be in to pay you cash money."

Ernie wanted to protest, but when he looked into Art Lee's eyes, he took a sudden change of heart. Cussing and fuming, he went back into the store.

"Miles," Lee said, "jump up on that horse and make sure he ain't goin' to start bucking before we put Shiloh on his back. I'll go inside, buy a few cigars and settle the bill."

Miles nodded, and as soon as the horse was roped and a bridle found, the cowboy grabbed the bay's mane and swung up on its back. The bay dropped its head and started bucking like crazy. Saddled, Miles might have had a chance, but bareback he lasted for about ten jumps and then went sailing into the air. He landed flat on his back and they all heard the air whoosh from his lungs. When the other cowboys rushed over to Miles, he was gasping for air like a fish out of water.

"The sonofabitch would happen to be a bucker!"

"A *hell* of a bucker!" another cowboy said.

"Who wants to have the next go at riding him?"

None of the cowboys did.

"I will," Shiloh said, figuring he had nothing to lose and maybe something to gain. "I'll ride him to a damned standstill."

"The hell you say! Miles is the best rider on the Lazy B payroll. If he can't ride that ornery bastard, you damn sure can't."

"Sure I can," Shiloh said. "I'm a better rider than Miles ever dreamed he could be."

The challenge was laid down and could not be ignored.

"Well, hoist his raggedy ass up on that bronc and then we'll tie his hands and ankles together and see just how good he really is," Joe said.

The Lazy B men exchanged glances. They all knew that they were sentencing Shiloh to almost certain death.

"Now wait a damned minute," Shiloh said. "That isn't fair."

"Nothin' in life is fair," Joe said, grabbing Shiloh. "Blindfold the horse and let's get this braggin' sonofabitch up there before Art comes back and puts the crimp on our fun."

In a moment, the cowboys had the bay blindfolded and Shiloh sitting on his back. They roped Shiloh's ankles together under the horse's belly.

"Hurry up before Art comes out!" one of the cowboys urged.

Shiloh could feel the half-broke gelding quiver with fear—or maybe he was the one that was scared half out of his wits. If he fell and got hung up under the horse, he would be a goner for certain. Shiloh knew that just one strike of a hoof could crack his skull like an eggshell.

They let the bay loose and at the same time whipped off its blindfold. Shiloh grabbed the reins with his right hand and drew them as short as he could while he grabbed a fistful of mane with his left hand. The bay squealed and tried to drop its head. Shiloh leaned back with all his might, attempting to keep the bay's head up. There had never been a horse able to buck well with its head high and this, he prayed, would not be the first.

The bay fought like crazy to drag its head down but Shiloh fought just as hard to keep it up. Shiloh was not the world's greatest rider, but he was good and, even more important, he was damned desperate. Kicking and fighting, hanging on for his life, he booted the young bay gelding in the ribs again and again until it quit trying to buck and chose to run. Running was what Shiloh had had in mind right from the start when he'd issued his brash challenge.

"Ya!" he shouted. "Ya!"

The bay was a brown streak with its tail flying straight out behind. Shiloh held on tight and let the gelding show its stuff as it raced off in a cloud of dust, leaving his captors far behind. Bullets crashed in the background and Shiloh could hear the shock and anger in the shouting Lazy B riders. He knew they'd be piling onto their own horses and taking up the chase, but he doubted any of them had enough horse to overtake this one.

"Ya!" Shiloh cried, urging the bay forward with a big grin on his face.

If he fell, he was a dead man, but if he'd not have escaped, he was a dead man anyway. Shiloh had no idea where he was going to run, but off to the north he could see some mountains. If he could just reach them, he might find someone who would untie him and trade him a very fast bay horse for a rifle or pistol. Armed and afoot, even though he had an aching ass and a bullet-bruised hip, he still liked his odds for survival.

18

IT WAS A horse race pure and simple and the stakes could not have been higher for Shiloh. As he galloped toward the distant hills, he concentrated on all the good things in his favor; there were not a lot of them, but he concentrated on them anyway. Firstly, the bay was a genuine racehorse and it seemed to have a lot of wind. Secondly, it was the fresher horse, the Lazy B animals having already put in a long day of hard riding. And finally, without a saddle, Shiloh figured he might average a few pounds lighter than the men who were falling behind. And when he had widened his lead to where it was well beyond rifle range, he slowed the bay to an easy jog, one that he hoped the animal could sustain until after sundown.

Suddenly, Shiloh had an entire new lease on life. Not that the odds weren't still very much against him, but he had always bucked and overcome long odds. Just before sundown he spotted a prospector's camp up ahead, but he veered wide and kept moving. The thing was, if the prospector was kind enough to cut Shiloh's ankles and wrists free, then he might be shot to death by the Lazy B riders. Besides, the hills up ahead looked like the kind that would entice a lot of prospectors, any one of which, under the cover of darkness, might be persuaded to help. When Shiloh glanced back over his shoulder into the twilight, all he could see was a cloud of dust rising toward a yellow moon.

He laughed and drew the bay to a walk so that it could catch its wind. About ten o'clock that night, he started climbing into the hills and almost at once saw the scattered campfires of prospectors. Shiloh headed for one of them, and when he drew near the fire, he called, "Hello the camp!"

The prospector had been sitting cross-legged in front of his campfire, and when Shiloh called, he twisted around suddenly and then dove for a rifle.

"Don't shoot!" Shiloh called. "I need help, not gold!"

The prospector was a large man with a bushy beard and wore an old flop hat. He stepped out of the firelight and moved toward Shiloh. "Who you be?"

"My name is Shiloh."

"What you be doing out ridin' around in the dark? Sneakin' up on a man when he was tryin' to cook his supper?"

"I wasn't sneaking," Shiloh said. He raised his bound wrists. "As you can see, I couldn't harm you even if I wanted to, which I don't."

When the prospector saw Shiloh's hands were bound, he became even more alarmed. He raised his rifle and pointed it at Shiloh's chest. "You a killer on the run?"

"No!" Shiloh gulped. "Well, actually I am sort of on the run, and I have killed a few men."

The prospector laid his cheek against the stock of his rifle and Shiloh could see him start to pull the trigger.

"Wait!" Shiloh cried. "I work on the same side of the law. I'm a bounty hunter."

"You're what?"

"A bounty hunter. I swear that I am!"

VENGEANCE TRAIL   131

"How do I know that? And if it were true, that still don't explain why you're all trussed up on that horse."

"I don't have much time to explain," Shiloh said, glancing back along his trail. "There are riders following me. All I ask is that you cut me free. Give me a chance to defend myself. You can do that much, can't you?"

"Why should I? I don't want no trouble. I don't want no part of whatever business you're up to. Just rein that horse around and ride!"

"But—"

The prospector didn't aim. He just pointed his rifle at Shiloh and fired. The slug passed so near to Shiloh's head that he swore he felt its breeze.

"Dammit!" Shiloh swore. "Now you've told them where I am!"

"Git!"

Shiloh wheeled his horse around and kicked it into a gallop. Art Lee and his riders would be along soon and they'd give the big prospector a hard time, but Shiloh doubted they'd kill the fool.

Shiloh decided not to head for the nearest camp, but set his course on one that appeared to be several miles to the northwest. He rode hard, driven by an urgency to get free and also by the trobbing pain in his still-aching behind.

As before, Shiloh hailed the camp, and this time there were two men who stepped out of the firelight with rifles in their fists. "State your business," the taller of the pair demanded.

"I'm in trouble," Shiloh said. "I've got five men chasing me. If I'm caught, I'll come to a bad end."

"Then maybe you deserve it," the other man said. "Either way, we don't want no trouble. We've already got all we can handle."

"Have you ever heard of the Lazy B ranch?"

The pair shook their heads.

"Well, it's owned by a ruthless old man whose son I had to kill in self-defense."

"Tell it to a jury," the taller man said. "We ain't interested."

"But I'll never live to see a jury!" Shiloh exclaimed. "And I'm not asking for nothing free except that you cut my wrists and ankles loose."

"Ah . . . I don't know," the shorter man hedged.

"Listen," Shiloh said, "if you found a suffering animal caught in a steel trap, you'd either put it out of its misery or you'd turn it loose. One way or the other. Well, either shoot me right now or cut me loose so I have a fighting chance."

The two miners exchanged glances and the taller one said, "He's right, Eb. I'm going to cut him free."

Eb nodded. "He looks pretty dangerous. Don't let him kick you in the head with them new boots he's wearin'."

"He tries that, he's a dead man."

"I won't try anything," Shiloh promised.

The tall man pulled a knife and cut the rope that bound his ankles. "Whoever did this wasn't playin' games. If you'd have fallen off . . ."

"I know," Shiloh said, cutting the man short. "Hurry with my wrists!"

When the ropes that bound Shiloh's wrists were severed, he heaved a deep sight of relief. He had already noticed that the tall man was carrying on old Navy percussion revolver that had been converted to use metallic cartridges. They were common and inexpensive. Not as good as Colt's later cartridge models, but still plenty accurate and reliable. Eb was holding a Winchester Model 1873, one of the best all-around rifles ever made. It was the fifteen-shot, twenty-four-inch barrel model that Shiloh favored for its superior accuracy over the shorter saddle carbine.

"Would you trade that rifle of yours for this horse and bridle?" he asked.

"Nope. Got no use for a horse," Eb replied.

Shiloh nodded, he'd expected the answer. If he'd been a miner, he'd much have preferred a good rifle, too.

VENGEANCE TRAIL

"What about you?" he asked the taller man. "Will you trade that old converted percussion pistol for this fine horse?"

"If I did that," the man said, "I'd be cheatin' you. Besides, I don't need a horse any more than Eb does."

Shiloh understood, but he desperately needed a weapon. "What about these new boots?"

"What about them?"

"I'll trade them to you for the pistol and those old clodhoppers you're wearing."

"Nope. These shoes I'm wearing might be old and ugly, but they're good for work."

"Yeah, but wouldn't it be nice to have a pair of handmade boots like these?"

"Sure. But I'd need a nice new Stetson too if I was going to shine."

Shiloh understood. He removed his new Stetson, which had cost him almost as much as the boots. "My new hat and boots for that pistol, your holster and all the ammunition you've got."

The tall man grinned. "Ain't that a deal though, Eb! I only paid twelve dollars for this old shooter and its holster."

"You do what you want," Eb said, "but do it quick. I don't cotton much to the idea of them riders bustin' in here and shootin' us along with him."

Shiloh stuck out his foot and the tall man yanked off his boot, then came around to the off side of his horse and yanked off the other. Shiloh whipped off his new hat and took the man's pistol, holster and cartridge belt.

"Got any more bullets?"

"Nope. But there's six in the gun and at least ten more in the belt. That ought to do 'er."

"Yeah," Shiloh said, strapping on the gun belt. He aimed the Colt at Eb. "Sorry, Eb, but I need to borrow your rifle."

Eb raised the Winchester and pointed it at Shiloh. "Over my dead body."

"That's your choice," Shiloh told the miner. "You see, odds are I'm going to die anyway. Now you, on the other hand, can loan me that rifle and get rich mining gold, or you can die. Either way, I'm going to count to five and then I'm going to shoot you right between the eyes if you don't give me that rifle."

Eb was so mad that Shiloh thought the miner was going to go crazy and open fire. The taller miner must have thought so too because he grabbed the rifle and tore it from his friend's hands.

"It ain't worth dying over, Eb!"

"The hell it ain't!" Eb cried, taking a swing at his companion, who pitched the rifle up to Shiloh and yelled, "Git!"

Shiloh caught the rifle and drove his heels into the bay's sweaty flanks. "I'll return the rifle if I kill 'em before they kill me!" he shouted as he raced off into the darkness.

Over the pounding hoofbeats of the bay, Shiloh could hear the two men fighting and shouting. He was sorry he'd had to do that to Eb, but his life was on the line, and when that was the case a man couldn't afford to play fair.

Shiloh turned the bay to the west and let it climb higher into the dark, treeless mountains. Come daylight, if the Lazy B men were still on his trail, he would start to whittle down the long odds.

19

TWO HOURS BEFORE dawn, Shiloh reined the exhausted bay up beside a mountain stream and let the animal drink. He slipped down from the horse feeling as if his legs were made of wood and his ass was full of splinters. Riding bareback was fun for a kid, but was hell for a grown man. His balls felt as big as duck eggs and his every step caused pain to shoot from his toes to the tips of his fingers. He had no food and he was lost.

Shiloh unbridled the bay and the animal staggered over to graze on the new spring grass that was just starting to appear along the waterway. He sat down on the bank and removed his shirt, then tore it in half. He used it and part of his reins to wrap his feet so that they didn't get cut to ribbons when he hiked up to a vantage point and looked to see if he was still being followed.

The hike took more out of him than he'd expected, but the bay needed feed and rest even worse than himself. If the animal failed, Shiloh knew he was finished for certain. At the top of a brushy hill, he raised up slowly and studied his back trail. He could see the five horsemen picking their way through the hills and around rocks, never losing his trail because the ground was still damp from snowmelt and the bay's hooves had left deep imprints.

Shiloh shook his head. He wished the Lazy B men would let it go, but he knew that old Horatio Ballock wouldn't allow that to happen. The men that followed him would either have to deliver Shiloh or just keep riding. Better for them, Shiloh thought, gripping the Model '73, that they should give up this unjust hunt.

Shiloh hunkered down on the hilltop. He could see the place where the riders would suddenly come into his range and where they'd be riding single file in a tight place among the rocks. It was there that he'd empty a few saddles and then see if the survivors had the stomach to keep coming.

Shiloh longed for a smoke but his tobacco was gone. He leaned back against a rock and closed his eyes for a minute, and almost instantly he felt a great drowsiness settle upon him. With a start, he raised his head and decided that he'd better keep his eyes wide open or he'd wake up staring into the muzzles of five revolvers—if he was allowed to wake up again at all.

Art Lee was in front and as the man slowly moved into the periphery of the Winchester's deadly range, Shiloh regretted that the foreman was the one that would have to die first. He'd been fair to Shiloh and not abusive like some of the other cowboys wanted to be.

"Maybe I'll just take you out of this scrape," Shiloh said, shifting his aim to the next man, the one that had taunted Shiloh about earning a reputation at his mortal expense.

Shiloh laid the barrel of the rifle across a rock and drew a bead on the young braggart. Slowly he squeezed the trigger, and when the rifle exploded Shiloh knew he'd killed the gunman with a slug through the chest. Shiloh did not waste even a split second in admiring his deadly work but put a bullet through Art Lee's right shoulder. He heard the foreman cry out in pain and saw him almost fall off his horse, then rein it about shouting for his men to take cover.

Shiloh got lucky. With only a few seconds left, he managed to plug a third rider before the man could escape. Only two of the five were able to reach cover unharmed.

"Go on back to the old man!" he hollered down at them. "Your fun is over. It's my turn if you keep coming after me!"

"Damn you!" Lee screamed. "I won't stop until one of us is dead!"

"Suit yourself!" Shiloh squatted down in the brush and could not resist yelling, "Got any tobacco and paper, Mr. Lee? I'm all out!"

His answer brought a swarm of bullets that ricocheted across the rocks. Shiloh grinned. He shouldn't have taunted them that way, but he was feeling damned pleased with his shooting just now. And then too, he was sore and tired enough that a little meanness was bubbling just under the surface. Shiloh took another peek over the rock. He could see the two dead men lying facedown on the trail, and the two that had got away clean were huddled beside Art Lee, probably trying to plug his bullet-riddled shoulder.

"Take him home to that old man!" Shiloh yelled. "Or better yet, go find a doctor!"

"In hell!" one shouted.

"Your choice, mister!"

Shiloh eased back from the rock and picked his way carefully down from the hilltop. When he returned to the bay and tried to bridle the beast, the animal was not one bit pleased. It tried to sink its yellow teeth into Shiloh's arm, but he smashed it across the muzzle and it reared back dragging him up in the air.

"Whoa, you jugheaded bastard!" Shiloh cried. "Just stand still!"

Shiloh got the horse bridled and then led it over to a rock, which he used to hop onto the animal's back. "Uggh," he groaned, not liking the feel of the bay's knobby backbone again as it split him up the middle. "Let's go. At least you got to eat for an hour or two. I'm so lean and hungry I could run down and eat the ears off a jackrabbit!"

The bay laid back its own ears to show that it was not pleased but Shiloh did not care. He would ride on until he found food and then he'd see if the three Lazy B men were still on his back trail. If they were, he'd lay another ambush and maybe get lucky enough to finish off the entire lot. Still, the fact of the matter was that Shiloh hoped the duo would turn around and cart Art Lee off somewhere to find a doctor. Doc Weaver would be fit enough by now to dig a slug out of the man's shoulder and save his life.

"That's what they really need to do," Shiloh told his bay gelding. "They need to hurry on back to Tuscorora and get Doc Weaver to take care of that man's shoulder. Otherwise, he's going to die. Ain't nothing that old man Ballock could do in this whole world that is worth dyin' for."

The bay's ears flicked forward and Shiloh saw a little shack about two miles up the trail. Maybe there he could find some food and even a little salve for the parts below his belt that were on fire. That would be real, real nice.

20

ART LEE HAD been shot once before, but that had been twelve years earlier and he didn't recall that it had hurt this bad. His shoulder felt as if someone had jammed a red-hot poker into it, and about the only good thing he could think about was that the bullet had passed on through and didn't have to be removed. Still, before he and his two remaining gunmen could get the shoulder patched, he'd lost plenty of blood.

"What are we going to do now?" Ben Hamilton asked nervously.

"We stay after the man until we get him!" Art snapped. "That's what the old man would want. That's why he's paying you big wages. Cowboys don't make a hundred dollars a month."

"Yeah," Ben growled, "well they don't get ambushed either. I'm pulling my freight."

Lee's voice shook with contempt. "If you run out now, either one of you, you'll be hounded to your graves. Ballock will hire detectives and gunfighters to hunt you down and kill you wherever you try to hide. There isn't a place that you can think of that he won't find you. And I'll help him, I swear it."

Ben exchanged glances with Jim, who never said much of anything, and what he did say was rarely worth hearing.

Ben pulled his six-gun and pointed it at the Lazy B foreman. "Art, if we shot you then no one would know what happened out here in these damned barren hills. What do you think of that idea, Jim?"

Jim spat a stream of tobacco and mused on the question in protected silence until Ben's patience wore out and he grated, "Dammit, what do you think!"

"I don't think so," Jim drawled.

"Why not?"

"Wouldn't be healthy."

"Well, neither is going after Shiloh!"

Art Lee looked up at his two men. He'd known that Ben was a snake and he'd never trusted Jim from the start. Now, they were talking about whether or not to kill him just as matter-of-factly as if they were discussing horses or the weather. It made Art think that it was time he changed bosses and climates. He'd worked too long and hard, been too loyal for too many years to end up like this—listening to a couple of killers decide his fate while he lay helpless with a hole in his shoulder.

"We can still get Shiloh," Art heard himself saying. "We can kill him and have this thing turn out just fine."

"How?" Ben asked, his gun still out.

"He won't be expecting that we'll keep coming after him. He'll think that he broke our nerve."

"Well, he about has!" Ben said. "In case you didn't notice, that man wasted damn few bullets killing Joe and Miles and wounding you in the bargain!"

"Shiloh is riding bareback without food. He has to stop soon. We'll catch him off guard the next time. I swear that we will. And Horatio told me before we left the ranch that he'd be giving us a thousand-dollar bonus when we brought Shiloh back to the ranch."

"Aw! You're just sayin' that!"

"No! I'm serious. He may be an ornery bastard, but Horatio's a man of his word. And you know how much he hates Shiloh. I tell you, there's a thousand dollars in this for us."

"Split even?" Jim asked, showing real interest now.

"That's right."

Ben grinned wickedly at Jim. "If we kill Art, we'd each get five hundred."

"If you kill me," Art Lee said, "you'll get nothing."

After a moment of tense silence, Jim finally drawled, "Let's give it another day, Ben."

Ben nodded and put his gun away. "All right. Can you ride, Art?"

Art Lee swallowed with relief. He'd thought he was going to be shot. "Sure," he breathed. "Just get me up on my horse."

They helped him back into the saddle and then they both mounted, and Ben said, "Art, you're going to lead the way. You're half dead now, so there's not as much to lose if you get plugged again."

Art did not share that opinion, but he gritted his teeth against the pain and took the lead. If Shiloh was waiting in ambush again just up ahead, a bullet might be a damned blessing.

Shiloh wasn't waiting. He was sitting at a table wolfing down beans just as fast as he could swallow. An old prospector sat on a nail keg across from him and watched with growing exasperation as Shiloh worked on his third heaping platter of food.

"Stranger, you're a mighty big eater. All them beans would have lasted me a week. They ain't cheap in this country and I hauled them in all the way from Bullion City."

With his mouth crammed with food, Shiloh mumbled, "I gave you a pretty fine Navy Colt in trade for all the beans I could eat, along with an old hat and a pair of boots not worth savin' for the dogs to chew."

"Yeah, well I didn't expect you'd eat that much!"

"Quit complaining. We made a deal. You just keep cooking until I've had my fill."

"You're worse than a damned hog with another man's food!"

"Ain't your food once you took my Colt in trade."

"Maybe I'll use it on you if you don't stop eating."

The Winchester was resting up against the table, and Shiloh's hand moved a little closer to it. "Old man, if you want to die, you get foolish and reach for that Navy Colt." The old man swallowed nervously and then he went to cook more food, muttering in anger to himself.

Shiloh finally had his fill and washed everything down with his fourth cup of strong coffee. He was dying for sleep but he'd made a decision. He was going to retrace his trail and see if he was still being followed. If he was, he'd force a showdown. Damned if he'd run any farther. Besides, the odds were now close to being even. Him against two healthy and one badly wounded man. Shiloh would take those odds any old day.

He hated to leave his Colt, for it had cost him plenty and he did not like this stingy old prospector. A decent fella would have fed a starving stranger and asked for nothing but a thank you. This stingy bastard wanted to wring everything he could out of Shiloh in the bargain.

"I hope you get shot through that belly of beans!" the ill-tempered old miner hollered as Shiloh mounted the bay.

In answer, Shiloh dropped the muzzle of his rifle across his saddlehorn, pointed it at a big copper kettle and shot a big hole through its center.

The old miner went crazy. "That kettle cost me five dollars, goddamn you!"

Shiloh laughed and reined the bay around, then drummed his heels to its flanks. He had not ridden fifty yards before the prospector opened fire with the converted Navy Colt. All the shots went ridiculously wide.

"Goddamn you," the prospector cried, "this gun don't even shoot straight!"

A tight grin formed on Shiloh's lips as he galloped on. It was a very good thing that he'd not depended upon that Navy Colt in the heat of a gunfight. He rode steadily for two hours, always stopping just on the low side of a ridge or hill and making sure that he had not been seen and in turn been set up for an ambush.

Very late in the afternoon, Shiloh was dismounting to lead his horse up a hill when, suddenly, he saw the three Lazy B riders top the hill not a hundred yards up ahead. For an instant, everyone froze. Shiloh recovered first. He threw the rifle to his shoulder and fired in one clean, unhurried but very rapid motion. A rider flipped over his saddle and a second one wheeled his horse around and went racing east as if chased by the devil himself.

That left Art Lee. Lee was all bent over the way a man sits when he's been shoulder- or rib-shot. Shiloh dismounted and levered another shell into his rifle.

"Give it up!" he yelled to the foreman of the Lazy B ranch.

But Art Lee shook his head. He yanked his rifle out of its scabbard and tumbled from his saddle into the brush. "It's just between you and me now, Shiloh!"

"It don't have to be this way. I'll let you go!"

"Ha!" Lee shouted. "The one important thing is that I won't let *you* go!"

Shiloh scowled with disappointment. It looked like he was going to have to kill Art Lee, who was the only man on the Lazy B payroll worth saving. He was about to try to change the foreman's mind when a bullet creased Shiloh's ear, spilling him to the dirt. Maybe punching Art Lee's ticket wasn't going to be quite as easy as he'd expected.

"Use your head!" Shiloh called, pulling his hand from his ear and seeing blood. "We don't need to kill one another."

"Sure we do!" Lee shouted. "If you don't come and get me, sooner or later I'll find you."

"You need a doctor, not another bullet."

"I'm coming after you," Lee shouted, standing up in plain view. "Are you man enough to stand up and face me?"

Shiloh levered another shell into the rifle and raised it to one knee. As soon as Lee saw him he opened fire with his six-gun, but he was shooting with the wrong hand and his aim was wild. But Shiloh's wasn't. He took aim and put a bullet right through Art Lee's chest. The Lazy B foreman spun around and then collapsed in a quivering heap.

"He wasn't as smart as he looked," Shiloh muttered to himself as he walked toward the fallen man. To his amazement, Art Lee was still alive when he reached the foreman's side. Shiloh knelt beside the dying man.

"I didn't want to kill you," Shiloh said, "but you gave me no damn choice."

"I know." Lee gripped Shiloh's arm hard. "Listen," he wheezed. "I want you to bury me deep. Don't want the coyotes to eat my body."

"You should have turned and rode away," Shiloh said. "I don't understand why the hell you didn't give up the fight."

Lee stared at him. "Shiloh, I got two thousand dollars buried in a bean can behind the ranch house. If you promise to keep the coyotes off my body, I'll tell you how to find it."

"The hell you say! How'd you come up with that kind of money?"

"Been savin' it for years," Lee whispered. "Was gonna start my own spread. Should have done . . . it!"

Shiloh stared at the man. "You wouldn't lie to me at a time like this, would you, Art?"

"No!"

Lee began to cough blood. Shiloh could see his eyes starting to glaze with death. Not wanting to lose the chance to dig up a small fortune, Shiloh shook Lee and said, "Art! Art, exactly where'd you put it? Tell me before you cash it in!"

"Swear you'll bury me deep!" the man gagged. "Swear it on your mother's grave!"

"On her grave," Shiloh vowed. "On my father's grave too! Now where is that money?"

Lee bent the crook of his index finger, motioning Shiloh closer. "It's . . . it's under the main house *shitter*."

Shiloh pulled back. "Come on! Nobody would bury his savings under a shitter!"

"I did because nobody would look there! And . . . and it ain't in the hole. Just to the right of it. Under the boards."

Lee's body began to spasm. "Bury me deep!"

Shiloh pulled back. "I will if you don't make me wait around too long. I'll be hungry again by tomorrow morning."

Art Lee managed to nod his head. His mouth worked silently and Shiloh looked away. He hated to see a man die so bad. He considered putting the man out of his misery with a bullet to the brain. While considering this, Shiloh reached into the man's shirt pocket and found the makings. He rolled himself a cigarette and inhaled deeply. The tobacco was harsh in his lungs and it snapped a weary haze from his mind. Shiloh smoked the cigarette down to nothing.

"Gone yet?" Shiloh asked, looking down at the foreman. To his considerable relief, Art Lee had breathed his last and the death rattle in his chest fell silent.

Shiloh buried him but it was hard without a shovel. The ground was rocky, and after a few minutes of scratching at it with a knife he found in Lee's boot, Shiloh decided to drag the dead ranch foreman over to an arroyo. Pulling him down to the bottom, he kicked and clawed at the banks of the arroyo until they caved in and covered the corpse.

Shiloh finished the distasteful job by piling rocks and brush over the body. "If there's a coyote out here hungry enough to go to all the work of reaching you," Shiloh said, "then I'm afraid he'll have earned the right to chew on your bloody bones. Without a pick or shovel, this is the best I could do, Art."

Shiloh climbed out of the arroyo and gathered up the Lazy B horses. He left the other body lying where it had fallen and then he turned his bay loose and climbed into Art Lee's saddle.

He would ride a few hours and try to overtake the one that had gotten away. If he did, good. If he did not, that was fine too. Either way, he was going after Art Lee's buried savings, and if that meant killing old Horatio Ballock to get it, that was just fine and dandy.

21

WHEN SHILOH APPROACHED Eb's camp, he raised the Winchester and fired it into the air. Eb and his big friend came rushing out.

"Brought your rifle back, Eb!" Shiloh called.

"Well I'll be a sonofabitch!" the prospector swore. "I'd have bet my burro that we'd never see you or that rifle again!"

Shiloh rode up and handed the rifle to the man. "I'm sorry I had to take it like that, but I'd have been a dead duck if the only thing I'd had to defend myself was that Navy Colt."

Eb nodded. "John and me saw those five men that was followin' you. They came by and they were real steamed up. They were a damned hard-nosed bunch. I can see why you needed a rifle and I can see what you musta done to 'em."

Eb and John were looking at the string of Lazy B horses that Shiloh was leading. Shiloh grinned. "If you see a horse you'd like, I'd still favor a trade to keep this Model '73, Eb. It saved my life."

"In that case, why don't you visit a spell. I can see that you've got a few Winchesters in those saddle scabbards."

"Them fancy boots and the Stetson don't fit worth a damn. Can't wear any of 'em," John complained.

"I'll give you your pick of rifles and gladly take back the boots and Stetson," Shiloh said, stepping down very gingerly. "I'm afraid I can't return your Navy Colt, I had to trade it for food and these lousy boots."

John grinned. The two prospectors invited Shiloh to spend the night, and he accepted and said, "I haven't had much sleep in a long time. I'd appreciate a good night's rest without worrying about someone sneaking up to put a bullet in me."

"Well, you don't have to worry about that in our camp," Eb said. "John and me ain't struck gold in so many years that folks just naturally stay away from us, if you understand what I mean."

"Sure," Shiloh said, "you two have bad luck so they stay away."

"That's right. But maybe havin' you spend the night here and getting these things will change our luck," Eb said.

Shiloh hoped so. That night he bundled up in his bedroll and slept like the dead, knowing that he could trust the two prospectors. In the morning, he shared their sourdough biscuits and some of their jackrabbit stew.

"I'll be leaving now," Shiloh said, pulling his new Stetson down snug after he'd resaddled the horses and tied them to a lead line. The boots felt good and he felt better. "I hope you boys strike it rich."

"I hope you don't get yourself killed at the Lazy B," Eb said with a look of real concern. "I could understand what you said around the campfire last night, but I doubt that any buried money is really hidden in the shitter like that dying man told you."

"To be honest," Shiloh admitted, "neither do I. But you know what? I'd always wonder and pretty soon it would drive me about half crazy. Might as well find out now one way or the other."

The two men nodded with understanding. They all shook hands and then Shiloh rode away leading his string of horses. On his way back, he spent a night in Tuscorora and visited Doc Weaver and his wife Edna. Both were in good health, and the doctor insisted that Shiloh step into his examination room and drop his pants.

"Uh-huh. Uh-huh," the doc murmured to himself as he pinched and prodded Shiloh's sore cheek.

"What does that mean?"

"It means that you've healed nicely, despite too much riding," the doc told him with reproach in his voice.

Shiloh pulled up his pants. "And I see that all those beautiful stitches I put in your gullet are gone."

"That's right," the doc said. "I got so many wrinkles that one little bitty scar or two is barely noticed."

To Shiloh's way of thinking, the scar was a lot more than "little bitty." It had healed nicely, but it was still an angry red line stretching almost from ear to ear. It made Shiloh realize what a miracle it was that the doc was still alive, and how fine a job he'd done with Edna's help and instruction.

"I wish," the doc said, "you weren't so insistent on going to the Lazy B after that supposed hidden cache of money. I doubt it's there and you'll just be riding into a hornets' nest."

"Oh," Shiloh drawled, "I'm not so sure of that. You see, Horatio Ballock lost his foreman and his best gunfighters when he sent 'em chasing after me. I doubt he's got much of anything left but a few hardworking cowboys. And cowboys, unless they're drunk, are not inclined toward gunfights. Most of them can't shoot worth a damn."

"But why even bother?"

"Two thousand reasons," Shiloh said with a wink. "That's plenty enough for me."

"What about the old rancher?"

"All I want is Art Lee's savings," Shiloh said. "The old man has lost enough to me already."

Doc Weaver was anything but pleased. "I still think you ought to let me see if I could get you enrolled in an eastern medical college."

"Why? So I could let everyone know for certain what they've always suspected—that I take to instructions about as well as a mule and that I'd fit into some college back there about as well as a polecat at a picnic?"

Doc Weaver chuckled. "Well," he conceded, "when you put it that way, I guess maybe you have a point."

"Damn right I do," Shiloh said, taking his leave.

He said good-bye to Edna, who held his hand tightly and whispered, "You saved my husband's life, Shiloh."

"We saved it, ma'am."

"Will you be coming through Tuscorora again?"

"I reckon I will in a week or so."

"Stop by and spend the night. I know a very lovely widow woman about your age. She's got golden hair, big blue eyes and she's a good church-going woman with three handsome little sons that need an honest, upright father."

"In that case, I'm disqualified," Shiloh said. "Anyway, I steer shy of good women. I like the other kind a whole lot better."

"You're a devil, Shiloh," the woman said, but there was no condemnation in her frail voice.

Shiloh finished his good-byes and then rode out. He was anxious to sell these extra Lazy B horses that were causing so much interest.

Shiloh sold the horses for about a quarter of what they were worth, and when he moved on to Chili Gulch, he saw that Isaac's livery was closed down. Shiloh remembered with more than a little bitterness how the old liveryman had been shot to death for trading stolen Lazy B horses and helping him in a time of need.

Remembering this, he rode up to the cemetery and found the old man's grave. It was pathetic and marked by nothing but a flimsy wooden cross. Shiloh knelt beside the grave and said, "It was my fault you ended up this way. I'll see that you at least get a decent headstone before I leave this part of the country. One engraved with your name."

With that, Shiloh remounted and set his sights on the Lazy B ranch shithouse. His intentions were to arrive in the dark of night, get the two thousand dollars and leave without a bullet being fired. But one thing for sure, if there was gun trouble, Horatio Ballock was going to be the first one to die.

22

SHILOH ARRIVED ABOUT ten o'clock that night and tied his horse back in the trees behind the ranch house. A full moon was shining and he could see the big shitter clearly. Being reserved for the ranch owner, it was much more commodious than most with two doors and probably had fancy seats and paper. Shiloh didn't care. A shitter was a shitter and this one attracted him only for the reason that Art Lee had pledged he would find money hidden under its boards.

Yes, and on the right side. Shiloh frowned. Facing the thing? Or sitting down using it? Oh well, he'd figure that one out quick enough. For two thousand dollars he would have torn the whole thing down and rebuilt it before dawn.

Shiloh had bought himself a hammer and a pry bar at the general store in Chili Gulch because he did not want to have to fumble around in the darkness looking for these tools in the Lazy B blacksmith shop. Now, as he crept forward, he caught the scent of the shitter and realized that he was going to have several very unpleasant minutes before he had Art Lee's money in hand.

Reaching the place, Shiloh stepped inside and started to close the door, but that cut off the moonlight and plunged him into a stinky darkness, so he left both doors open wide. Wrinkling his nose and steeling his resolve, he set right to work. As expected, there were real handmade seats instead of just holes in the boards, and they had to be pried off before he could proceed.

Unfortunately, the seats were nailed down in about twenty places each, and Shiloh had a hell of a time getting them off. Cussing, gagging with the stench and making a lot more noise than he wanted, Shiloh finally removed both seats and, out of pure spite, dropped them down the holes. If Ballock prized the damn things enough to go after them they were his again.

Now the cross boards. They were thick because Ballock and his son were big men. Shiloh had to really work to pull them up. He was certain that Art Lee had devised an easier way to get to his money, but damned if he had either the time or patience to figure it out. As the boards lifted, Shiloh almost lost his stomach because the stench was so strong. Finally, though, and with not too much screeching of nails in protest, he did remove the two heavy front planks.

To his delight, he saw a big tin can resting just beside the hole. Shiloh reached down inside it and felt money! He pulled the can up and removed a thick roll of greenbacks. A big grin covered his face as he stepped outside to see that most of them were tens and twenties. Shiloh didn't know if there was actually two thousand dollars in the roll or not, but it was more money than he'd seen in one place in a hell of a while.

Shiloh pocketed the money. "Thanks, Art!"

"Hold it!"

Shiloh's fists streaked for the guns on his hips. They came up fast and exploded in his fists even as he felt a bullet pluck his arm. He spun and lost his balance, backpedaling into the shitter, knowing that he had drilled Horatio Ballock twice in the gut.

Shiloh almost crashed through the remaining seat boards and fell into the stinking hole. Arms waving wildly, he somehow managed to save himself. A moment later, he jumped out of the shitter and quickly sprinted for his horse. Shiloh could hear the confused shouts of the cowboys, and even though they might be poor shooters, there were more of them than he cared to brace.

Shiloh reached his horse, tore the reins free and vaulted into the saddle. Whipping his horse forward through the brush and the trees, he was almost beheaded by a low-hanging branch. It knocked his new Stetson off and set his head to spinning.

Hell, he thought, giving his horse its head to choose its own path of flight, let some poor Lazy B cowboy find the Stetson and consider it his lucky day. Shiloh hoped he'd be wearing it when they planted old Horatio Ballock six feet under the cold, hard ground.

Shiloh made a quick stop in Chili Gulch and that was at the undertaker's business. "How much does a good headstone cost?"

"How good?"

Shiloh was feeling expansive with two thousand dollars in his pants. "The best."

"Fifty dollars—with engraving."

"Fine," Shiloh said, dragging out the thick roll of greenbacks. "Got a paper and pencil?"

The undertaker nodded, looking disappointed because he figured he could have asked for and received a lot more than fifty dollars given the size of Shiloh's roll of bills.

Shiloh scribbled a note. "Have this engraved on Isaac's headstone."

"Isaac who?"

"The old man who owned your livery stable," Shiloh snapped. "Hell, man! You buried him less than a month ago!"

"Oh, yes, of course. Isaac Potter."

"Yeah," Shiloh said. "Now read it out loud for me."

"Sir?"

"I said *read* the damned thing!"

The undertaker read the message. *"Isaac—they paid in full."*

He glanced up at Shiloh with a confused expression. "Sir, I don't understand."

"It ain't important that you do," Shiloh said, heading for the door, "because—if there's a life in a hereafter—Isaac Potter will know what it means and be glad."

America's new star of the classic western

GILES TIPPETTE

author of *Hard Rock, Jailbreak* and *Crossfire* is back with his newest, most exciting novel yet...

SIXKILLER

Springtime on the Half-Moon ranch has never been so hard. On top of running the biggest spread in Matagorda County, Justa Williams is about to become a daddy. Which means he's got a lot more to fight for when Sam Sixkiller comes to town. With his pack of wild cutthroats slicing a swath of mayhem all the way from Galveston, Sixkiller now has his ice-cold eyes on Blessing—and word has it he intends to pick the town clean.

Now, backed by men more skilled with branding irons than rifles, the Williams clan must fight to defend their dream—with their wits, their courage, and their guns....

Turn the page
for an exciting preview of
SIXKILLER
by Giles Tippette

Coming in May from
Jove Books

IT WAS LATE afternoon when I got on my horse and rode the half mile from the house I'd built for Nora, my wife, up to the big ranch house my father and my two younger brothers still occupied. I had good news, the kind of news that does a body good, and I had taken the short run pretty fast. The two-year-old bay colt I'd been riding lately was kind of surprised when I hit him with the spurs, but he'd been lazing around the little horse trap behind my house and was grateful for the chance to stretch his legs and impress me with his speed. So we made it over the rolling plains of our ranch, the Half-Moon, in mighty good time.

I pulled up just at the front door of the big house, dropped the reins to the ground so that the colt would stand, and then made my way up on the big wooden porch, the rowels of my spurs making a *ching-ching* sound as I walked. I opened the big front door and let myself into the hall that led back to the main parts of the house.

I was Justa Williams and I was boss of all thirty thousand

deeded acres of the place. I had been so since it had come my duty on the weakening of our father, Howard, through two unfortunate incidents. The first had been the early demise of our mother, which had taken it out of Howard. That had been when he'd sort of started preparing me to take over the load. I'd been a hard sixteen or a soft seventeen at the time. The next level had jumped up when he'd got nicked in the lungs by a stray bullet. After that I'd had the job of boss. The place was run with my two younger brothers, Ben and Norris.

It had been a hard job but having Howard around had made the job easier. Now I had some good news for him and I meant him to take it so. So when I went clumping back toward his bedroom that was just off the office I went to yelling, "Howard! Howard!"

He'd been lying back on his daybed, and he got up at my approach and come out leaning on his cane. He said, "What the thunder!"

I said, "Old man, sit down."

I went over and poured us out a good three fingers of whiskey. I didn't even bother to water his as I was supposed to do because my news was so big. He looked on with a good deal of pleasure as I poured out the drink. He wasn't even supposed to drink whiskey, but he'd put up such a fuss that the doctor had finally given in and allowed him one well-watered whiskey a day. But Howard claimed he never could count very well and that sometimes he got mixed up and that one drink turned into four. But, hell, I couldn't blame him. Sitting around all day like he was forced to was enough to make anybody crave a drink even if it was just for something to do.

But now he seen he was going to get the straight stuff and he got a mighty big gleam in his eye. He took the glass when I handed it to him and said, "What's the occasion? Tryin' to kill me off?"

"Hell no," I said. "But a man can't make a proper toast with watered whiskey."

"That's a fact," he said. "Now what the thunder are we toasting?"

I clinked my glass with his. I said, "If all goes well you are going to be a grandfather."

"Lord A'mighty!" he said.

We said, "Luck" as was our custom and then knocked them back.

Then he set his glass down and said, "Well, I'll just be damned." He got a satisfied look on his face that I didn't reckon was all due to the whiskey. He said, "Been long enough in coming."

I said, "Hell, the way you keep me busy with this ranch's business I'm surprised I've had the time."

"Pshaw!" he said.

We stood there, kind of enjoying the moment, and then I nodded at the whiskey bottle and said, "You keep on sneaking drinks, you ain't likely to be around for the occasion."

He reared up and said, "Here now! When did I raise you to talk like that?"

I gave him a small smile and said, "Somewhere along the line." Then I set my glass down and said, "Howard, I've got to get to work. I just reckoned you'd want the news."

He said, "Guess it will be a boy?"

I give him a sarcastic look. I said, "Sure, Howard, and I've gone into the gypsy business."

Then I turned out of the house and went to looking for our foreman, Harley. It was early spring in the year of 1848 and we were coming into a swift calf crop after an unusually mild winter. We were about to have calves dropping all over the place, and with the quality of our crossbred beef, we couldn't afford to lose a one.

On the way across the ranch yard my youngest brother, Ben, came riding up. He was on a little prancing chestnut that wouldn't stay still while he was trying to talk to me. I knew he was schooling the little filly, but I said, a little impatiently, "Ben, either ride on off and talk to me later or make that damn horse stand. I can't catch but every other word."

Ben said, mildly, "Hell, don't get agitated. I just wanted to give you a piece of news you might be interested in."

I said, "All right, what is this piece of news?"

"One of the hands drifting the Shorthorn herd got sent back to the barn to pick up some stuff for Harley. He said he seen Lew Vara heading this way."

I was standing up near his horse. The animal had been worked pretty hard, and you could take the horse smell right up your nose off him. I said, "Well, okay. So the sheriff is coming. What you reckon we ought to do, get him a cake baked?"

He give me one of his sardonic looks. Ben and I were so much alike it was awful to contemplate. Only difference between us was that I was a good deal wiser and less hotheaded and he was an even size smaller than me. He said, "I reckon he'd rather have whiskey."

I said, "I got some news for you but I ain't going to tell you now."

"What is it?"

I wasn't about to tell him he might be an uncle under such circumstances. I gave his horse a whack on the rump and said, as he went off, "Tell you this evening after work. Now get, and tell Ray Hays I want to see him later on."

He rode off, and I walked back to the ranch house thinking about Lew Vara. Lew, outside of my family, was about the best friend I'd ever had. We'd started off, however, in a kind of peculiar way to make friends. Some eight or nine years past Lew and I had had about the worst fistfight I'd ever been in. It occurred at Crook's Saloon and Cafe in Blessing, the closest town to our ranch, about seven miles away, of which we owned a good part. The fight took nearly a half an hour, and we both did our dead level best to beat the other to death. I won the fight, but unfairly. Lew had had me down on the saloon floor and was in the process of finishing me off when my groping hand found a beer mug. I smashed him over the head with it in a last-ditch effort to keep my own head on my shoulders. It sent Lew to the infirmary for quite a long stay; I'd fractured his skull. When he was partially recovered Lew sent word to me that as soon as he was able, he was coming to kill me.

But it never happened. When he was free from medical care Lew took off for the Oklahoma Territory, and I didn't hear another word from him for four years. Next time I saw him he came into that very same saloon. I was sitting at a back table when I saw him come through the door. I eased my right leg forward so as to clear my revolver for a quick draw from the holster. But Lew just came up, stuck out his hand in a friendly gesture, and said he wanted to let bygones be bygones. He offered to buy me a drink, but I had a bottle on the table so I just told him to get himself a glass and take advantage of my hospitality.

Which he did.

After that Lew became a friend of the family and was important in helping the Williams family in about three confrontations where his gun and his savvy did a good deal to turn the tide in our favor. After that we ran him against the incumbent sheriff who we'd come to dislike and no longer trust. Lew had been reluctant at first, but I'd told him that money couldn't buy poverty but it could damn well buy the sheriff's job in Matagorda County. As a result he got elected, and so far as I was concerned, he did an outstanding job of keeping the peace in his territory.

Which wasn't saying a great deal because most of the trouble he had to deal with, outside of helping us, was the occasional Saturday night drunk and the odd Main Street dogfight.

So I walked back to the main ranch house wondering what he wanted. But I also knew that if it was in my power to give, Lew could have it.

I was standing on the porch about five minutes later when

he came riding up. I said, "You want to come inside or talk outside?"

He swung off his horse. He said, "Let's get inside."

"You want coffee?"

"I could stand it."

"This going to be serious?"

"Is to me."

"All right."

I led him through the house to the dining room, where we generally, as a family, sat around and talked things out. I said, looking at Lew, "Get started on it."

He wouldn't face me. "Wait until the coffee comes. We can talk then."

About then Buttercup came staggering in with a couple of cups of coffee. It didn't much make any difference about what time of day or night it was, Buttercup might or might not be staggering. He was an old hand of our father's who'd helped to develop the Half-Moon. In his day he'd been about the best horse breaker around, but time and tumbles had taken their toll. But Howard wasn't a man to forget past loyalties so he'd kept Buttercup on as a cook. His real name was Butterfield, but me and my brothers had called him Buttercup, a name he clearly despised, for as long as I could remember. He was easily the best shot with a long-range rifle I'd ever seen. He had an old .50-caliber Sharps buffalo rifle, and even with his old eyes and seemingly unsteady hands he was deadly anywhere up to five hundred yards. On more than one occassion I'd had the benefit of that seemingly ageless ability. Now he set the coffee down for us and give all the indications of making himself at home. I said, "Buttercup, go on back out in the kitchen. This is a private conversation."

I sat. I picked up my coffee cup and blew on it and then took a sip. I said, "Let me have it, Lew."

He looked plain miserable. He said, "Justa, you and your family have done me a world of good. So has the town and the county. I used to be the trash of the alley and y'all helped bring me back from nothing." He looked away. He said, "That's why this is so damn hard."

"What's so damned hard?"

But instead of answering straight out he said, "They is going to be people that don't understand. That's why I want you to have the straight of it."

I said, with a little heat, "Goddammit, Lew, if you don't tell me what's going on I'm going to stretch you out over that kitchen stove in yonder."

He'd been looking away, but now he brought his gaze back to me and said, "I've got to resign, Justa. As sheriff. And not only that, I got to quit this part of the country."

Thoughts of his past life in the Oklahoma Territory flashed through my mind, when he'd been thought an outlaw and later proved innocent. I thought maybe that old business had come up again and he was going to have to flee for his life and his freedom. I said as much.

He give me a look and then made a short bark that I reckoned he took for a laugh. He said, "Naw, you got it about as backwards as can be. It's got to do with my days in the Oklahoma Territory all right, but it ain't the law. Pretty much the opposite of it. It's the outlaw part that's coming to plague me."

It took some doing, but I finally got the whole story out of him. It seemed that the old gang he'd fallen in with in Oklahoma had got wind of his being the sheriff of Mategorda County. They thought that Lew was still the same young hellion and that they had them a bird nest on the ground, what with him being sheriff and all. They'd sent word that they'd be in town in a few days and they figured to "pick the place clean." And they expected Lew's help.

"How'd you get word?"

Lew said, "Right now they are raising hell in Galveston, but they sent the first robin of spring down to let me know to get the welcome mat rolled out. Some kid about eighteen or nineteen. Thinks he's tough."

"Where's he?"

Lew jerked his head in the general direction of Blessing. "I throwed him in jail."

I said, "You got me confused. How is you quitting going to help the situation? Looks like with no law it would be even worse."

He said, "If I ain't here maybe they won't come. I plan to send the robin back with the message I ain't the sheriff and ain't even in the country. Besides, there's plenty of good men in the county for the job that won't attract the riffraff I seem to have done." He looked down at his coffee as if he was ashamed.

I didn't know what to say for a minute. This didn't sound like the Lew Vara I knew. I understood he wasn't afraid and I understood he thought he was doing what he thought was the best for everyone concerned, but I didn't think he was thinking too straight. I said, "Lew, how many of them is there?"

He said, tiredly, "About eighteen all told. Counting the robin in the jail. But they be a bunch of rough hombres. This town ain't equipped to handle such. Not without a whole lot of folks gettin' hurt. And I won't have that. I figured on an argument from you, Justa, but I ain't going to make no battlefield out of this town. I know this bunch. Or kinds like them." Then he raised his head and give me a hard look. "So I don't want no argument out of you. I come out to tell you what was what because I care about what you might think of me. Don't make me no mind about nobody else but I wanted you to know."

I got up. I said, "Finish your coffee. I got to ride over to my house. I'll be back inside of half an hour. Then we'll go into town and look into this matter."

He said, "Dammit, Justa, I done told you I—"

"Yeah, I know what you told me. I also know it ain't really what you want to do. Now we ain't going to argue and I ain't going to try to tell you what to do, but I am going to ask you to let us look into the situation a little before you light a shuck and go tearing out of here. Now will you wait until I ride over to the house and tell Nora I'm going into town?"

He looked uncomfortable, but, after a moment, he nodded. "All right," he said. "But it ain't going to change my mind none."

I said, "Just go in and visit with Howard until I get back. He don't get much company and even as sorry as you are you're better than nothing."

That at least did make him smile a bit. He sipped at his coffee, and I took out the back door to where my horse was waiting.

Nora met me at the front door when I came into the house. She said, "Well, how did the soon-to-be grandpa take it?"

I said, "Howard? Like to have knocked the heels off his boots. I give him a straight shot of whiskey in celebration. He's so damned tickled I don't reckon he's settled down yet."

"What about the others?"

I said, kind of cautiously, "Well, wasn't nobody else around. Ben's out with the herd and Norris is in Blessing. Naturally Buttercup is drunk."

Meanwhile I was kind of edging my way back toward our bedroom. She followed me. I was at the point of strapping on my gunbelt when she came into the room. She said, "Why are you putting on that gun?"

It was my sidegun, a .42/40-caliber Colts revolver that I'd been carrying for several years. I had two of them, one that I wore and one that I carried in my saddlebags. The gun was a .40-caliber chambered weapon on a .42-caliber frame. The heavier frame gave it a nice feel in the hand with very little barrel deflection, and the .40-caliber slug was big enough to stop any thing you could hit solid. It had been good luck for me and the best proof of that was that I was alive.

I said, kind of looking away from her, "Well, I've got to go into town."

"Why do you need your gun to go into town?"

I said, "Hell, Nora, I never go into town without a gun. You know that."

"What are you going into town for?"

I said, "Norris has got some papers for me to sign."

"I thought Norris was already in town. What does he need you to sign anything for?"

I kind of blew up. I said, "Dammit, Nora, what is with all these questions? I've got business. Ain't that good enough for you?"

She give me a cool look. "Yes," she said. "I don't mess in your business. It's only when you try and lie to me. Justa, you are the worst liar in the world."

"All right," I said. "All right. Lew Vara has got some trouble. Nothing serious. I'm going to give him a hand. God knows he's helped us out enough." I could hear her maid, Juanita, banging around in the kitchen. I said, "Look, why don't you get Juanita to hitch up the buggy and you and her go up to the big house and fix us a supper. I'll be back before dark and we'll all eat together and celebrate. What about that?"

She looked at me for a long moment. I could see her thinking about all the possibilities. Finally she said, "Are you going to run a risk on the day I've told you you're going to be a father?"

"Hell no!" I said. "What do you think? I'm going in to use a little influence for Lew's sake. I ain't going to be running any risks."

She made a little motion with her hand. "Then why the gun?"

"Hell, Nora, I don't even ride out into the pasture without a gun. Will you quit plaguing me?"

It took a second, but then her smooth, young face calmed down. She said, "I'm sorry, honey. Go and help Lew if you can. Juanita and I will go up to the big house and I'll personally see to supper. You better be back."

I give her a good, loving kiss and then made my adieus,

left the house, and mounted my horse and rode off.

But I rode off with a little guilt nagging at me. I swear, it is hell on a man to answer all the tugs he gets on his sleeve. He gets pulled first one way and then the other. A man damn near needs to be made out of India rubber to handle all of them. No, I wasn't riding into no danger that March day, but if we didn't do something about it, it wouldn't be long before I would be.

If you enjoyed this book, subscribe now and get...

TWO FREE

A $7.00 VALUE–

If you would like to read more of the very best, most exciting, adventurous, action-packed Westerns being published today, you'll want to subscribe to True Value's Western Home Subscription Service.

Each month the editors of True Value will select the 6 very best Westerns from America's leading publishers for special readers like you. You'll be able to preview these new titles as soon as they are published, *FREE* for ten days with no obligation!

TWO FREE BOOKS

When you subscribe, we'll send you your first month's shipment of the newest and best 6 Westerns for you to preview. With your first shipment, two of these books will be yours as our introductory gift to you absolutely *FREE* (a $7.00 value), regardless of what you decide to do. If you like them, as much as we think you will, keep all six books but pay for just 4 at the low subscriber rate of just $2.75 each. If you decide to return them, keep 2 of the titles as our gift. No obligation.

Special Subscriber Savings

When you become a True Value subscriber you'll save money several ways. First, all regular monthly selections will be billed at the low subscriber price of just $2.75 each. That's at least a savings of $4.50 each month below the publishers price. Second, there is never any shipping, handling or other hidden charges—*Free home delivery*. What's more there is no minimum number of books you must buy, you may return any selection for full credit and you can cancel your subscription at any time. A TRUE VALUE!

A special offer for people who enjoy reading the best Westerns published today.

WESTERNS!

NO OBLIGATION

Mail the coupon below

To start your subscription and receive 2 FREE WESTERNS, fill out the coupon below and mail it today. We'll send your first shipment which includes 2 FREE BOOKS as soon as we receive it.

Mail To: **True Value Home Subscription Services, Inc. P.O. Box 5235
120 Brighton Road, Clifton, New Jersey 07015-5235**

55773-690

YES! I want to start reviewing the very best Westerns being published today. Send me my first shipment of 6 Westerns for me to preview FREE for 10 days. If I decide to keep them, I'll pay for just 4 of the books at the low subscriber price of $2.75 each; a total $11.00 (a $21.00 value). Then each month I'll receive the 6 newest and best Westerns to preview Free for 10 days. If I'm not satisfied I may return them within 10 days and owe nothing. Otherwise I'll be billed at the special low subscriber rate of $2.75 each; a total of $16.50 (at least a $21.00 value) and save $4.50 off the publishers price. There are never any shipping, handling or other hidden charges. I understand I am under no obligation to purchase any number of books and I can cancel my subscription at any time, no questions asked. In any case the 2 FREE books are mine to keep.

Name _____

Street Address _____ Apt. No. _____

City _____ State _____ Zip Code _____

Telephone _____

Signature _____
(if under 18 parent or guardian must sign)

Terms and prices subject to change. Orders subject to acceptance by True Value Home Subscription Services, Inc.

Classic Westerns from
GILES TIPPETTE

Justa Williams is a bold young Texan who doesn't usually set out looking for trouble...but somehow he always seems to find it.

__BAD NEWS 0-515-10104-4/$3.95

Justa Williams finds himself trapped in Bandera, a tough town with an unusual notion of justice. Justa's accused of a brutal murder that he didn't commit. So his two fearsome brothers have to come in and bring their own brand of justice.

__CROSS FIRE 0-515-10391-8/$3.95

A herd of illegally transported Mexican cattle is headed toward the Half-Moon ranch—and with it, the likelihood of deadly Mexican tick fever. The whole county is endangered... and it looks like it's up to Justa to take action.

__JAILBREAK 0-515-10595-3/$3.95

Justa gets a telegram saying there's squatters camped on the Half-Moon ranch, near the Mexican border. Justa's brother, Norris, gets in a whole heap of trouble when he decides to investigate. But he winds up in a Monterrey jail for punching a Mexican police captain, and Justa's got to figure out a way to buy his brother's freedom.

For Visa, MasterCard and American Express orders ($10 minimum) call: 1-800-631-8571

FOR MAIL ORDERS: CHECK BOOK(S). FILL OUT COUPON. SEND TO:	POSTAGE AND HANDLING: $1.50 for one book, 50¢ for each additional. Do not exceed $4.50.
BERKLEY PUBLISHING GROUP 390 Murray Hill Pkwy., Dept. B East Rutherford, NJ 07073	BOOK TOTAL $ _____
NAME_____	POSTAGE & HANDLING $ _____
ADDRESS_____	APPLICABLE SALES TAX $ _____ (CA, NJ, NY, PA)
CITY_____	TOTAL AMOUNT DUE $ _____
STATE_____ ZIP_____	PAYABLE IN US FUNDS. (No cash orders accepted.)
PLEASE ALLOW 6 WEEKS FOR DELIVERY. PRICES ARE SUBJECT TO CHANGE WITHOUT NOTICE.	